(Excellent
balancing)

GENIUS IDEAS (mostly)

Liz Pichon

Wafer balancing (new sport)

SCHOLASTIC

Scholastic Children's Books
An imprint of Scholastic Ltd
Euston House, 24 Eversholt Street
London, NW1 1DB, UK

Registered office: Westfield Road, Southam,
Warwickshire, CV47 0RA
SCHOLASTIC and associated logos are trademarks and/or
registered trademarks of Scholastic Inc.

First published in the UK by Scholastic Ltd, 2012
This edition published 2019

ISBN 978 1407 19346 5

Printed by CPI Group (UK) Ltd, Croydon, CR0 4YY
Papers used by Scholastic Children's Books are
made from wood grown in sustainable forests.

1 3 5 7 9 10 8 6 4 2

www.scholastic.co.uk

To my sister

Who made me EXCELLENT toys, bought lovely books and showed me how to draw with fancy pens and crayons.

Lyn
×× ♥

→ Fancy crayons

Beddy Byes

↗ (This card was a bit annoying, though)

THIS is a

GENIUS idea...

A FLIP BOOK
in a book. Watch the
bug dance

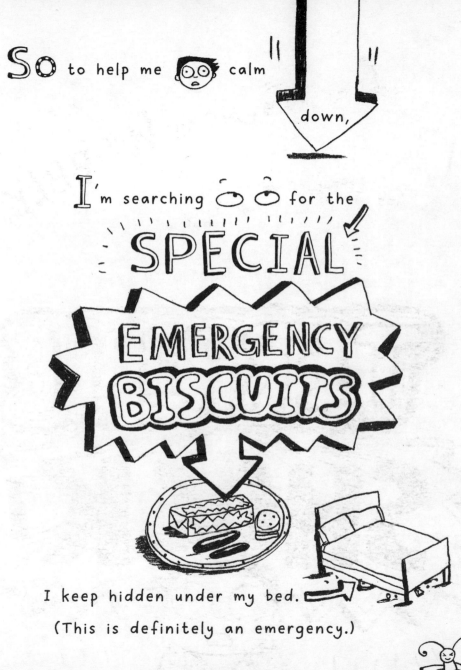

So to help me calm down,

I'm searching for the

SPECIAL

EMERGENCY BISCUITS

I keep hidden under my bed.

(This is definitely an emergency.)

biscuit crumbs

PHEW! That's better.

OK, let me explain what happened. I was in the bathroom, pretending to have a shower while reading my comic (like you do).

When SOMEONE started **KNOCKING** really **loudly** on the door. I assumed it was my sister Delia ...

... so I ignored her.

4

Then she did it again ...

... and again ...

... and again.

Knock

Knock

Knock

Knock

The noise was very annoying. But I managed to carry on reading EVERY single page of my comic REALLY slowly. EVENTUALLY when I'd finished, I very CAREFULLY opened the bathroom door.

I was expecting Delia to SHOUT at me for taking so long. I wasn't expecting to see this.

Grrrrrrr

It was a HORRIBLE Sight! I let out a LOUD

ARGH!

Which made Dad 😠 come running out of the bedroom to see what all the **noise** was about. He said, "What's the problem here?" 😠 So I said, "Delia's the problem. She **looks** **SCARY** without her 👓 ← sunglasses!"

Then Dad said it would be **nice** to have just ONE morning without being (disturbed) by the two of us **⚡ARGUING.** 😠

Delia got **REALLY CROSS** and pointed at ME, saying I was the only one who was "DISTURBED". **Then** she told Dad that he looked

 totally ridiculous.

Before disappearing into the bathroom and

 slamming the door.

Which left me in

FULL VIEW

of what Dad was wearing.

I couldn't decide who looked WORSE:

Delia without her sunglasses or Dad in his cycling shorts ? Mum wasn't much help either. She came upstairs and

SHOUTED, "Why is everyone shouting?"

Followed quickly by "And what on EARTH are you wearing?" Dad pointed out that she was the only one who was shouting and the cycling shorts were all part of his

Carefully planned new fitness regime.

Which made Mum LAUGH out loud.

ha! ha! ha!

I decided that this was probably a good time to head back to my room because:

NASTY SURPRISES + SHOCKS = EMERGENCY BISCUITS

It's a good job I keep a few hidden for these kinds of situations. I just hope there are no more unwanted surprises today. Sigh... I eat half of the (second) emergency wafer and start to imagine what MY idea of a FUN AND VERY RELAXING day at school would be. Mmmmmmm ... I think it would probably go something like this...

M r Fullerman is DELIGHTED to see me (even though I'm late).

Hello, Tom, VERY good to see you.

I have my own special COMFY chair and table that are as far away as possible from that very annoying M arcus M eldrew.

Marcus

sneaky snack box

far away

comfy chair

Lessons are OPTIONAL so I can choose
what I want to do (which is easy).

Choose Your LESSONS Today

ART	✗
MATHS	✓
Doodling	✗
MUSIC	✗
Spelling	
FUN Experiments	✓

Our NICE new art teacher
Miss Straw
insists I do a WHOLE
art project on ...

CARAMEL WAFERS.

Really? If you insist — I have *✻ ✱ fun ✱ arranging them
into towers before spending as MUCH time as
I want drawing and doodling.
Miss Straw is VERY

Sigh

impressed — Well done, Tom! — and lets
me eat TWO wafers for my snack.
AND I'm allowed to unwrap the others and use
the foil for my interesting wafer collage.

(The wafers I can save to eat later.)

Miss Straw thinks I am an ART BISCUIT GeNiuS.

I agree.

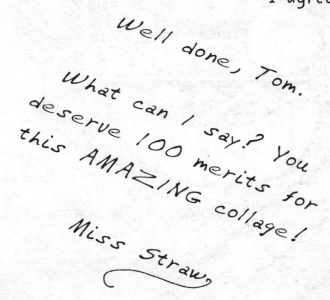

Well done, Tom.

What can I say? You deserve 100 merits for this AMAZING collage!

Miss Straw,

(I show my 100 merits to Marcus, which annoys him.)

Then the day gets even better. A few friends and I have a DELICIOUS lunch served by ...

... the teachers.

More iced water, Tom?

TEACHERS' TABLE

I eat in the best part of the dinner hall (for a change). I'm allowed to have SECONDS of pudding, followed by a relaxing rest with my feet up before the next lesson starts.

Which is

EXTRA FUN EXPERIMENTS.

(Outside – because it would be SUNNY ☀

on my perfect day.)

The whole class helps me place hundreds of

WAFERS in a l o n g row around the

school. Then I get to PUSH the first

wafer forward, causing them all to fall one by

one in an AMAZING pattern

(like dominoes).

Solid

Amy Porter

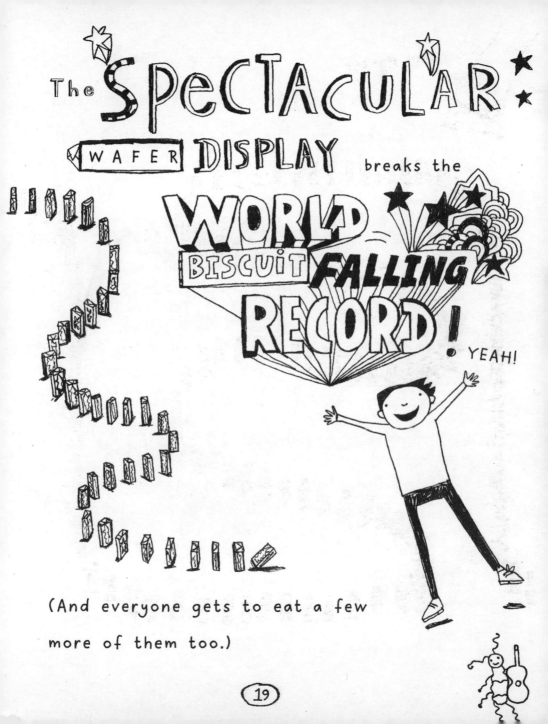

The SPECTACULAR

WAFER DISPLAY breaks the

WORLD BISCUIT FALLING RECORD!

YEAH!

(And everyone gets to eat a few
more of them too.)

Then as a **special** treat, **M**r Fullerman
announces that our MUSIC LESSON ♫
today will be taught by ...
DUDE 3, only the **BEST BAND** EVER!
Who arrive at our school
in their fancy ↕ HUGE
tour bus. They put on a fantastic
concert for the entire school, and because Derek
(my best mate) and I are **DUDE 3**'s
BIGGEST fans, we get to stand on
stage and play along with our own guitars
to all the songs ♫♫ that we know.
DUDE 3 congratulate **US** on how good
WE are. Which makes **M**arcus
pull a face like this: Huh?

But that's NOTHING ...

compared to the LOOK on Delia's face

when DUDE 3 pull up outside

OUR house in their tour bus.

Then me and Derek

get out, saying, (Later, Dude3)

to the whole band,

who wave back.

Then we carry our BRAND

NEW COOL guitars that the band have

given us back to the house.

Now THAT'S MY idea of the BEST and MOST AMAZING DAY at school EVER!

Oh well... You never know. Today might turn out to be a GOOD day after all? Like LAST WEEK in assembly (which I wasn't looking forward to), Mrs Nap asked everyone a question.

Who can tell me what month it is and what year?

Before I could put UP my hand to answer, Marcus Meldrew practically LEAPT off the floor, waving his arm around, so Mrs Nap would pick him. She did.

But the REALLY funny bit was when Mrs Nap asked Marcus to sit down and he accidentally said LOUDLY,

Yes, Mummy.

Then he couldn't understand why we were all LAUGHING so much. Mrs Nap had to say,

> I think you meant to say
> YES, Mrs Nap.

It was HILARIOUS!
I laughed a LOT that day.
Right __NOW__, though, if Mum and Dad see how late I am, I'll be in trouble.

Although I'm not sure they'd notice. I can still hear Mum chuckling EVERY time she says the words fitness regime like it's the FUNNIEST joke she's EVER heard.

There's a good chance that he could start turning up at my school, or WORSE STILL, my friends' houses, wearing something EVEN more embarrassing than those BRIGHT BLUE CYCLING SHORTS.

IF THAT'S POSSIBLE?

I slip downstairs and grab some breakfast and realize that I am properly late for school now. Mum is upstairs and still a bit busy.

I could go and ask her to write me a nice LATE NOTE to give to

ha! ha!

(Mum being busy)

Mr Fullerman, which would probably stop me from getting into any trouble?

OK, TOM

But why bother when it's SO much easier ...

... just to write one myself.

(A genius idea.)

Dear Mr Fullerman,

<u>Poor</u> Tom has had a VERY nasty shock this morning due to his ~~rotten stupid~~ sister scaring him. I'm very sorry he's late for school. His sister has been warned not to scare him again (or else).

Because of his SHOCK, Tom might find it hard to concentrate on any tricky maths today. Just letting you know.

Thank you,

Rita Gates

There, all done!
(Hopefully Mr Fullerman won't suspect

anything dodgy about my note. I didn't mention

Dad's shorts, as that would take too long

to explain.)

Dad comes downstairs and starts doing some

weird kinds of stretching

moves.   Mum is SHOUTING from

upstairs to me:

Have you gone yet, Tom?

So I say BYE to Dad quickly and remind him I

might be going to Norman's house for a band

practice tonight. He says, "Norman's house

isn't too far. How about I *run* over and

collect you?" And I say,

"NO WAY!"

just that little bit too quickly in case he
decides to turn up looking like ...

well, like that.

I tell him Derek's dad is coming to pick us up.

"All sorted, no need to worry, Dad."

Good thinking ...

phew!

Derek's not waiting outside: he's already left for school. So I set off with my SPECIAL LATE NOTE safely in my bag.

As I walk past the shop, I'm thinking maybe I could POP in for a small snack? (Good idea.) It takes me a while to choose what to have.

But because I have a LATE NOTE, I'm hoping Mr Fullerman will read it and say, That's all fine, Tom then let me off the hook.

And if he doesn't, at least I'll have my snack to eat.

Fingers crossed.

mmmmm?

FRUIT CHews

When I finally arrive at school, no one is around. It's **REALLY** quiet **EVERYWHERE.** Apart from Mrs Nap's classroom, where I can hear some odd noises *wafting* out of her slightly open door.

It sounds a bit like ... CATS Yowling iN PAIN.

Owww {w} ww

Awwwww

I go and take a sneaky 👁 👁 peek
to see what's going on.

It is Mrs Nap.

She seems to be Singing

the WHOLE register?

Worse than that, Mrs Nap is making
the class sing their names back to her.
One by one. Which is PAINFUL
to hear.

Charlie Smith?

Charlie Smith
is here,
Mrs Nap

Mrs Nap is being her usual
cheerful self when she sings.

"Isn't this FUN, everyone?"

And Charlie Smith (who's just sung his name)

sings back, "NOOOOO, not really."

Which makes Mrs Nap a bit CROSS.

So she sings, "Oh dear ... let's sing

it again from the beginning and this time

we'll ALL do it properly."

Charlie Smith tries to sing,

"I was only joking, Mrs Nap!"

But it's too late.

Luckily for me (and my class) Mr Fullerman

doesn't do "register singing". I think we'd be

there ALL day if he did.

I'm SO busy peering in the classroom that I don't hear Mrs Mumble behind me until she says,

Hello, Tom.

Which makes me JUMP.

"Shouldn't you be in class?"

I explain I was on the way there and I have a LATE NOTE. SPECIAL Mrs Mumble remembers there's a "special buddy talk this morning. Mr Fullerman was taking your class to meet some of the younger children."

So I say, "Great."

And I'm about to go off and find them.

Then she adds, "But I'm not sure WHICH class they've gone to. Best you wait in the school office with ⌐me⌐ until they're back so I can mark ✓ you in the register. We don't want you just wandering round school, do we?"

(Me wandering)

I'm (thinking...

1. What IS a "buddy talk"?
2. How long will I have to sit in the school office for, as it can be a *BIT* awkward?

What are you doing here, Tom

Mrs Mumble points to a seat and asks me
not to talk while she makes an announcement
over the loudspeaker.
At least this should be
fun to watch.

Mrs Mumble clears her throat
and LEANS into the speaker
while pushing a special RED button.
As soon as she starts speaking, her voice
goes all, well ...

Mumbly.

"Attention, OAKFIELD School, can I remind EVERYONE that this Friday it's **Teacher Training** Day, so school will be finished **ONE HOUR** earlier than usual."

I can just about hear *CHeers* coming from all over the school (which is funny).

"This lunchtime's chess club is cancelled due to an **EXTRA** rehearsal for Dancing Through the Decades with Mrs Nap."

Another slightly smaller *CHeer* goes around.

Then she finishes by telling everyone...
"One more thing. When Mr Fullerman returns to his class, could he send someone to collect **TOM GATES** from the school office, as he was **LATE** for school and is waiting in the office to be **COLLECTED**. Thank you."

huh?

GREAT, now the **WHOLE** school knows I'm late. **AND** Mrs Mumble has made me sound like I'm some kind of **PARCEL**.

(Groan.)

TOM GATES
(For collection)
THIS WAY UP

As Mrs Mumble's finished her message, I MUST remind her about my LATE NOTE so I don't get into trouble.

I say, "Mrs Mumble, I know I'm LATE but I have a NOTE to explain why."

And she says, "That's good, Tom. I'd like to SEE that note."

Which makes me PANIC a bit.

My note is stuffed into my bag and I can't find it anywhere.

I put my bag down on to her desk so I can have a good rummage around. While I'm looking, I carefully explain ALL about my OLDER sister Delia

and how she gave me a NASTY SHOCK this morning (which is true, she did). But I don't say what happened. Instead I recreate my "I'M SHOCKED!" face like this...

Which startles Mrs Mumble a bit.

And because I STILL can't find my note, I carry on...

39

"It's in here somewhere."
Then I tell Mrs Mumble how Mum
was a bit worried about me
because I looked slightly PALE.

"Mum told me I was CLAMMY
from the SHOCK and I needed to sit down
and recover a bit before going to school.
Which is why I'm late, Mrs Mumble."
I do a slightly different type of face ... like
this...

Then breathe a SIGH of relief,
as I've just found my note. I give it to Mrs
Mumble, who's about to read
it when there's a
KNOCK at the office door.

LATE note

Hello!

It's **AMY PORTER** from my class. She tells **Mrs Mumble** TWO things.

1. I can come back to class, as **Mr Fullerman** is there now.

I'm back

2. The **WHOLE** school have just heard my (why I'm LATE) explanation because the

LOUDSPEAKER is still on.

IT IS?

Mrs Mumble **LIFTS** my bag off the SPECIAL red button and says,

"Oh dear, that'll be why."

I'm doing a "**VERY** embarrassed" face, which looks like this...

Shame

Groan.

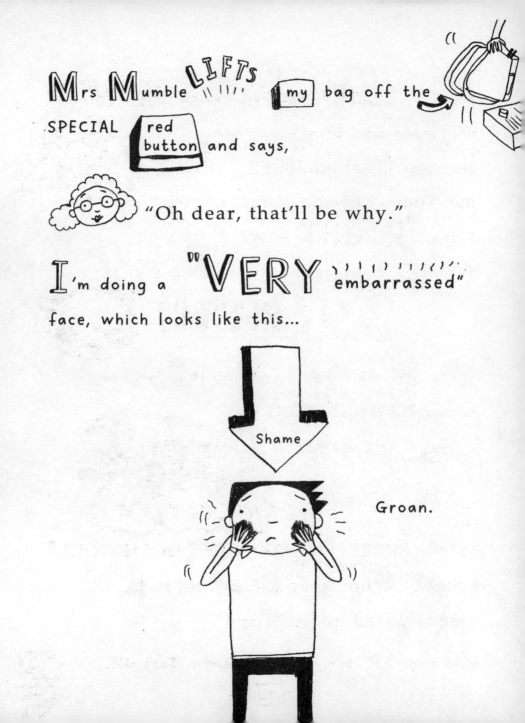

And if **that's** not bad enough, Mrs Mumble

only goes and brings out her

She says, "That reminds

me, Tom – I need a picture of you."

I say, "RIGHT NOW?"

Because I can feel my face going even

REDDER!

Mrs Mumble tells me that it's for the

school NEWSLETTER.

"You have a

SPECIAL
MENTION

for the EXCELLENT DRAWING HOMEWORK*

on your school book. Nothing to be

embarrassed about, Tom!"

*See page 357, Everything's Amazing (Sort Of).

Which **cheers** me up a bit. **I**'d forgotten about being in the NEWSLETTER.

At least **AMY** will see that I don't make stupid mistakes like this *all* the time. Speaking of stupid mistakes...

Mrs **M**umble is just about to take the photo when someone else **knocks** at the door. There's a kid standing outside with a COMB ... ... STUCK in his hair.

Mrs Mumble looks at him and says, "How did you do that?"

The kid says he's not really sure.

Mrs Mumble tells him to Wait there, then goes ahead and takes what I hope will be a VERY Nice picture of me for the NEWSLETTER.

SMILE

Now Mrs Mumble's got this kid with a comb stuck in his hair to deal with, my LATE NOTE seems to have ⟋Slipped her notice, which is a

BIG RELIEF.

Phew

On the way back to class, AMY PORTER wants to know exactly what Delia did that gave me such a SHOCK. I can't say "She took off her sunglasses, it was terrible" because that doesn't sound shocking at all. (Even though it was.)

Instead I say, "It was nothing, I'm over it now." (Like I'm being brave.)

Then I manage to quickly change the subject by asking **AMY** what the **BUDDY TALK** was all about. **AMY** says the **YOUNGER** kids get to choose an older kid (one of us) to be their **BUDDY.**

"We have to look out for them and make sure they're happy in school. That kind of thing. **Mr Fullerman** took us to say **hello** so the little kids know who we all are now." I say, "Lucky them."

Since I wasn't there, I ask AMY what happens if you don't get chosen to be a buddy. AMY tells me,

"Not all the little kids want to have buddies. So don't worry, it will be less hassle for you not to be picked."

But I think I'd make a good BUDDY. I could show them all kinds of really important stuff, like:

° How to be first in the lunch queue.

sneaky short cuts

Oh yes!

B̲ack in class, M̲r F̲ullerman says,

Better late than NEVER, Tom.

I̲ don't have to explain where I've been because everyone has already heard. (Groan.)

M̲arcus Meldrew can't WAIT to tell me how STUPID I sounded over the loudspeaker.

You sounded stupid

So I tell him,

"You don't need a LOUDSPEAKER to SOUND STUPID."

And he says, "No one will pick you as a buddy because you weren't there."

So I (think) quickly and say,
"No one will pick YOU as a buddy
because you WERE there."

Then Mr Fullerman GLARES at
both of us and says,

STOP TALKING.

Which shuts Marcus up ... for now.

Mr Fullerman says today he's going to
read us a STORY. (I'm hoping this means
we'll have a nice

RELAXing

day after all?)

Then he adds...

"**Listen** carefully, as we'll be doing some work about the story later."

Mr Fullerman holds up a book (Groan...) and asks if anyone has heard of

Aesop's Fables?

And **M**ark **C**lump, who hardly EVER puts his hand up, gets VERY EXCITED and says,

> Mr Fullerman, I HAVE, I HAVE. They're my _favourite_.

Mr **F**ullerman asks Mark,

> **Which is your FAVOURITE FABLE, Mark?**

And Mark Clump thinks for a while...
(Quite a long while, actually.)

Mr **F**ullerman looks impressed that Mark is thinking about his answer SO carefully.

U ntil he says...

P lain if it's t(O)asted with [butter]

and [jam] ... yum.

Which isn't quite the answer
Mr Fullerman was expecting.

The class start LAUGHING Ha! Ha!
                           Ha!
                           Ha!
because we've just realized Mark thinks
Mr Fullerman said BAGEL.

Whoops

So just to make it clear for everyone,

Mr Fullerman says,

The FABLE –
NOT BAGEL, FABLE –
I'll be reading is called
"THE BOY WHO CRIED WOLF".

Marcus nudges me and says he knows this

story already.

The wolf eats the boy in the end ... that's it, really.

Thanks for telling me the

ending, Marcus.

That's just great.

The good news is Marcus has given me 😊 an idea 💡 for a doodle. I carefully arrange a few innocent-looking books on my desk.

While Mr Fullerman is reading out the story, I get busy drawing.

AMY is watching 😊 and smiling. I have to keep stopping to pay attention to Mr Fullerman.

(Me paying attention.)

Marcus has been ignoring me. Until right at the end of my drawing, when I do a 😖 picture of him ...

... that catches his eye.

Marcus has only gone and put his

hand **UP** and interrupted

Mr **F**ullerman, who's not very happy.

⟵ He tells **M**r **F**ullerman,

"**Sir! Tom Gates**
is drawing, **SIR.**"

Luckily for me, **M**r **F**ullerman doesn't tell

me off. I just have to put down my pen

and **LISTEN.**

Which I do (for a while).

But Marcus is **still** watching me.

Which is annoying.

So I start to draw this line

Hey!

| Marcus | ➡️ |

Yes, **YOU.** Follow this line

61

Don't stop looking!

keep watching

this LINE, YOU are

If you are

following

STILL

AN IDIOT!

Ha!

Ha!

Ha!

Ha!

Ha!

Marcus looks like this now.

(I should try this trick
on Delia too!)

Break-Time
(at LAST)

My best mate Derek ⟹ comes to find me. He can't come to band practice tonight, which is a shame.

"I have to go to Aunt Julia's house with my mum." Derek looks really fed up.
"I hope she doesn't do that face-squeeze thing on me again.
It's embarrassing."

Look at you!

⟵ Aunt Julia

To make Derek feel better, I tell him about when my Aunty Alice, Uncle Kevin and the cousins came round for a family barbecue last weekend.

Derek says, "I **LOVE** barbecues."
And I say, "**So** do I, usually."

I explain to Derek,

"It would have been OK, but Dad
was in a **REALLY BAD** mood, mostly
because of Uncle Kevin and his dodgy jokes.

Eating for
two?

AND he didn't like my

paper banger either, or the

noise it made. Then when Dad

dropped all the sausages on the

ground, he said it was **MY** fault!"

Derek says, "I was wondering where Rooster got those sausages from. **And** what's a paper banger*?"

I still have a paper banger **Scrunched** up in my pocket. **S**o I take it out and try and smooth out the creases to make it work better. It's not great, but it does the trick.

I tell Derek, "I was only showing the cousins how to make it go **BANG!**

Like this ... by flicking it over my head..."

BANG

*See page 308 on how to make a paper banger.

$\mathbb{D}$erek seems to have cheered up
a bit and wants to have a go at making the
paper banger work himself.

It takes a few tries,

duff

but eventually Derek gets
it at the right angle

Bang!

... to make a very loud

BANG!

The noise attracts a bit of attention from some of the little kids in school, who come over and want to know

What's that?

"It's a paper banger," I tell them. "Look."
Then I show them how it works.
"You can make them yourself, it's easy."

BANG!

This kid called **Joey** wants to take a closer look. He's the one I saw in the school office with the comb stuck in his hair (which is out now).

I'm very nice and let **Joey** have a go. I show him the knack of making the banger work properly too. **W**hich is a mistake...

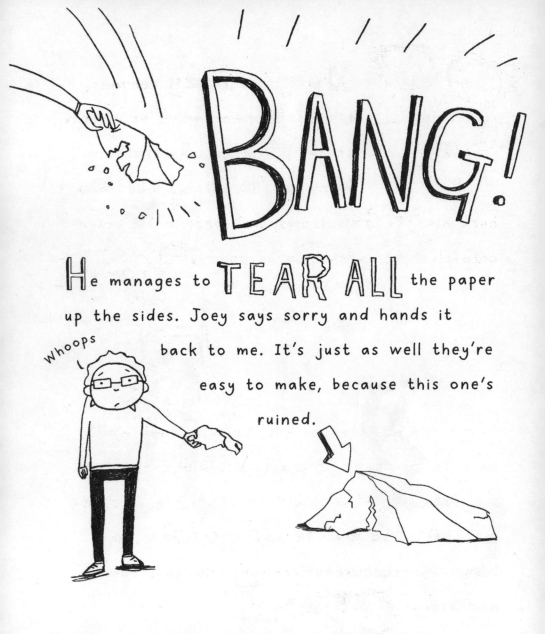

BANG!

He manages to **TEAR ALL** the paper up the sides. Joey says sorry and hands it back to me. It's just as well they're easy to make, because this one's ruined.

Whoops

Derek says **Joey** reminds him of **N**orman when he breaks stuff. **M**ind you, ever since **N**orman fell off his bike* and hurt his 🖐 ← elbows, he's been a bit more careful about everything he does.

Mind that banana skin

Derek reminds me to tell Norman that we'll have to cancel band practice tonight. He suggests, "We could do it at the weekend instead?" **A**nd then he says **AGAIN**, "You won't forget to tell Norman, will you, Tom?" And I say, As if!

* See page 247 of Everything's Amazing (Sort Of) for the full story.

PE

(Stands for Physical Education, or in Norman's case, Poorly Elbows.)

Even though Norman is the FIRST person I see when I come into class, I completely forget to tell him about band practice. Norman gets to miss PE because of his elbows.

I ask him if he's being allowed to relax for a bit or do something else? Norman points to some worksheets and tells me, "Mr Fullerman wants me to catch up with these. He says the class have done them already."

We have?

I take a quick look, but I don't remember doing ANY of these worksheets? I'll keep quiet and won't mention it in case Mr Fullerman wants me to catch up as well.

Tom!

Norman has to go and sit in the **school office** with Mrs Mumble

Ready, Norman?

(Groan.)

(like I did), while the rest of class 5F follow Mr Fullerman for PE.

Follow me!

We get changed and go outside to the playing fields, as the weather is nice and **WARM.**

Mr Fullerman announces to the class that we're about to have

LOTS of FUN!

And we all cheer! "YEAHHH!"

Then he adds,

Training for our SPORTS DAY!

Which makes us go... "Awwwwwwwwwww."

Training doesn't sound like much fun to me?

Mr Fullerman tells us to (Warm Up)

by running round the field ➡ (once.)

Solid (who's [not] keen on running) puts up his hand and says, "Mr Fullerman, I am really WARM already, so do I have to run?"

I think Solid has made a VERY good point.

So I say, "Sir, I'm VERY WARM too. Phew!..."

In the hope Mr Fullerman might change his mind about making us do all that running.

NO chance.

Mr Fullerman says,

TWICE round the playing fields for EVERYONE.

Ignoring both of us.

The whole class are GROANING now and staring at us. Apart from Brad Galloway, who loves running. Yes!

"

"

Florence Mitchell's not happy.

She says,

Nice work, Tom.

Whoops...

Like it's ALL MY FAULT!

Mr Fullerman is keeping his BEADY EYES on ME the WHOLE time I'm running. I can't even hide behind a TREE or pretend to be doing up my shoelaces for a quick *REST* without him shouting,

"Keep going, TOM ... I can SEE YOU!"

I'm REALLY **HOT** and I've gone **BRIGHT RED** now.

Solid can hardly SPEAK he's

SO PUFFED out.

He (just about) says,

"We've ... hardly ... started ... yet."

Which is true. (Groan.)

Marcus Meldrew comes over to ME

and starts WAVING his hands

around my head. (Which is annoying.)

I say, "What are you doing, Marcus?"

And he says,

"**My** hands are **COLD**, I'm just warming them up ...

ON YOUR FACE!"

Ha! Ha! **HA! HA!**

Marcus thinks he's **HILARIOUS.**

I think it's going to be a VERY **long PE** lesson.

Groan.

My class, 5F, have never (I repeat) NEVER won ANYTHING on SPORTS DAY. We're a bit rubbish compared 😕 to some of the other classes.

Every year at the end of SPORTS DAY Mr Fullerman says,

"WELL DONE, Class 5F, you've ALL done SO WELL! Just remember, it's the taking part that counts."

(Even though we've come last.)

While Mr Sprocket's class, Class 5S, are usually

* ★ Celebrating ★ ...

84

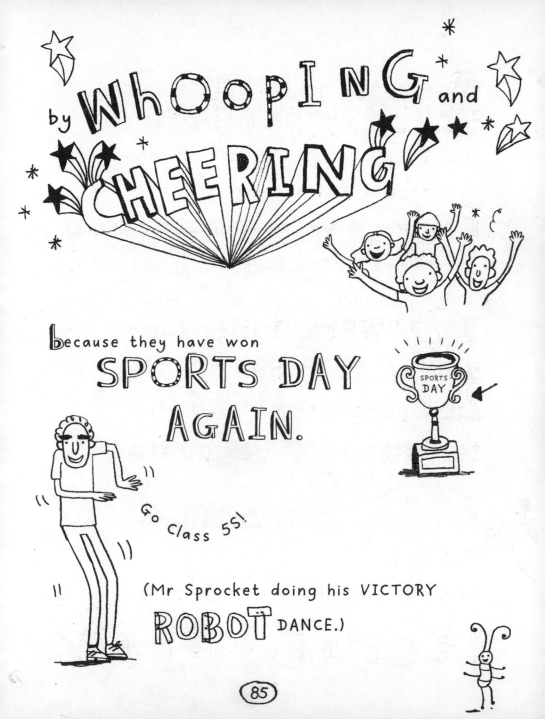

by WHOOPING and CHEERING

because they have won
SPORTS DAY
AGAIN.

Go class 5S!

(Mr Sprocket doing his VICTORY ROBOT DANCE.)

SPORTS DAY

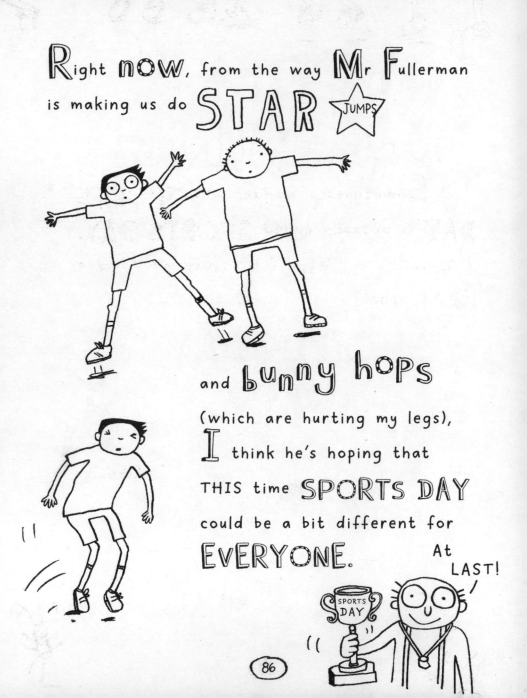

Right **now**, from the way **Mr Fullerman**
is making us do **STAR** JUMPS

and **bunny hops**
(which are hurting my legs),
I think he's hoping that
THIS time **SPORTS DAY**
could be a bit different for
EVERYONE.

At LAST!

SPORTS DAY

86

Sometimes I wonder why SPORTS DAY is actually called SPORTS DAY. I'm not sure EVERYTHING we do is a REAL sport?

Like...

Hula Hooping

Which is a LOT harder than it looks.

Skipping

Mr Fullerman says boxers skip to keep fit.
But they probably don't have someone like
Marcus standing RIGHT NEXT to them messing
up THEIR skipping
ROPE all the time.

Beanbag juggling

BEANBAGS get used a LOT on SPORTS DAY:

we do loads of throwing and catching

and running in between them.

My personal favourite is beanbag balancing.
It's fun to put them on your _____ arms,
knees, or do a double balance on your

knee

and

foot at the same time.
I often pile them on my
head. Mr Fullerman tells me to
stop when I get to about here.

The **LONG** jump is the only "sport"
we do today that I've seen 👁 👁 on [telly.]
Mr Fullerman wants all of us to have a go.
He tells us,

"**You need a good _run_ up,**
then throw ━ your 🏃 legs
forward and jump into the sandpit."

Marcus starts bending his legs up and
down. **I** say, "What are you doing,
Marcus?" and he says, "I'm getting
ready to do a **VERY BIG**
jump, because I am really good at
long jump." Now he's taking deep
breaths as well (which is a bit odd).

Solid says to me, "Maybe he is good at long jump after all?"

I say, "Let's see."

We watch Marcus as he starts to **RUN** as fast as he possibly can towards the sandpit...

Then he LEAPS into the air and does a really really ...

... small   jump.

**Good try, Marcus.
Stretch your legs
out next time.**

Now Marcus thinks he's done a

BRILLIANT jump.

(He hasn't.)

Mr Fullerman finishes off our training session with what he says is a WARM DOWN.

Solid says the warm down is making him even HOTTER.

On the way back to school, I can hear Marcus telling ANYONE who'll listen that he is a natural at long jump. (He's not.)

Brad Galloway is doing that funny thing when you walk behind someone really closely and they don't know you're there. He's right behind Solid, copying everything he does. Solid doesn't notice for ages, until I tell him. He says, Good joke, Brad and wants to try it on someone else now.

Trouble is, Solid's a bit TALL and noisy and his shadow keeps giving him away.

I know you're there, Solid

Hello, Solid

When we get back to school, Mr Fullerman asks us to help put away the "sports equipment" (I think he means the beanbags, hula hoops and skipping ropes).

Then he takes the opportunity to remind us how little time there is before SPORTS DAY.

Like we didn't already know.
He says,

Team 5F, you are all going to do AMAZINGLY well this year, I can tell... Blah blah blah

But it's hard to concentrate when I can see THIS. PTO

Brad is going crazy behind Mr Fullerman's
back.

I'm trying not to laugh, but it's almost
impossible! Everyone who can see Brad dancing
starts laughing too.
Mr Fullerman gets a bit cross and says,

"This is NO laughing matter, Class 5F!"

Ha! Ha!

Ha!

Ha!

Ha!

Ha!

Ha!

Ha! Ha!

Ha!

Because he can sense something is going on behind his back. Then Mr Fullerman spins round SUPER FAST, just in time to catch Brad Galloway .,

... doing absolutely **nothing**.

Hello, sir

(Lucky escape or what?)

Mr Fullerman says, **"I'll be keeping a close eye on YOU, Brad."**

Which is excellent news for <u>ME</u>, because (in between doing some work) I've been trying to finish my **SUPER LARGE** doodle in class.

Which is tricky to do with **M**r **F**ullerman STARING at me (like he does).

I can't **WAIT** until lunchtime to catch up with Norman and Derek and tell them **ALL** about how **BRAD** was dancing behind **Mr Fullerman's** back.

In the dinner hall, I stand up to show them EXACTLY what he did. Like this: "I am very busy **WAFTING** my arms around over my head and from side to *side*, recreating Brad's dance. I don't even **NOTICE** that DEREK is making a funny face at me.

I carry on and say, "Trust me ... it was **REALLY** funny! Especially when **Mr Fullerman** was going **ON** and **ON** about SPORTS DAY

100

and Brad Galloway was wobbling his legs about like this..."

Then I tell them that the **BEST** part of all was that

Mr Fullerman had ABSOLUTELY NO idea what Brad was doing behind his back.

Derek nudges me and says...

"I think he does now."

Because Mr Fullerman is looking over in MY direction with his **BEADY** eyes and shaking his head in a very STERN and disapproving way. I have a horrible feeling that he's heard everything I've just said.

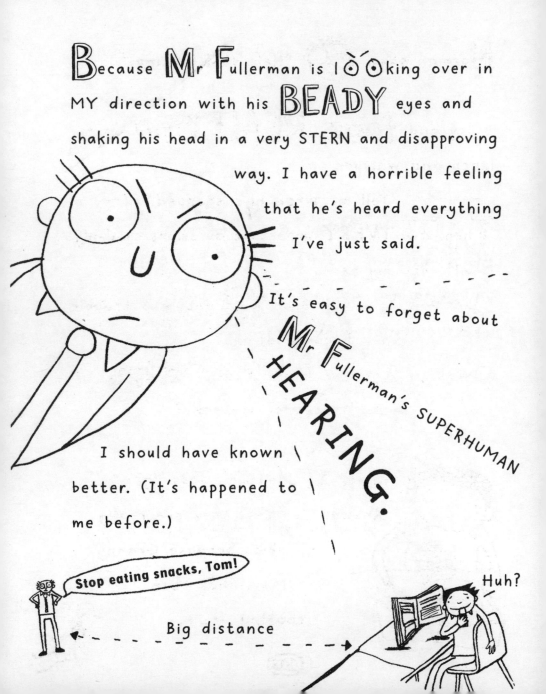

It's easy to forget about Mr Fullerman's SUPERHUMAN HEARING.

I should have known better. (It's happened to me before.)

Stop eating snacks, Tom!

Big distance

Huh?

Norman says, "He's still looking."

I try and focus REALLY hard on my
lunch and whisper,

"Tell me when he's stopped."

Then two VERY important questions suddenly
'POP' into my head.

Question 1. Will Brad get into trouble
because of me?

Question 2. Are those REALLY chips
on top of my cake?

Answer 1. Mmmmm, possibly?

Answer 2. Yes, they are really
chips because Granny
Mavis has been
cooking again.

I manage to carefully pick out the chips and eat the cake (the two don't usually go together unless you're Granny Mavis). Norman seems keen to eat my chips, which is fine by me (but a bit weird).

Yum

Then while he's eating, I ask Norman what it was like missing PE and having to do his work in the school office. And he says it was all right. But he did find out something interesting. And Derek and I both say, WHAT'S that?

Norman tells us that he overheard a conversation in Mr Keen's office with Mrs Mumble.

He says, "They were both talking about **BANDS**."

"Really?"

Chips

Norman carries on, "I was being very quiet and not moving around much so I could listen. I heard Mr Keen say,

Norman NOT moving

"If we can get **DUDE 3** to play for the school, that would be GREAT. The children would enjoy seeing them."

And I say,

"Are you sure?" And Norman says with a mouthful of chips,

Yes, I'm sure.

Derek wonders why **DUDE 3** would want to play at OUR school? If it DOES turn out that **DUDE 3** are playing in our school, that would be...

BRILL

AMA

FANTAST

Derek warns me that I shouldn't get TOO

EXCITED

"I mean, Norman's not totally sure Mr Keen said **DUDE?** . He might have got it wrong. No offence, Norman," Derek adds.

"None taken," Norman says.

But it's true. Norman does get stuff muddled up sometimes.

Oh?

I said bring a PEN, Norman.

TOY HEN

We're getting ready to leave the dinner hall when we hear a MASSIVE CRASH!

It's a BIG vegetable accident with a WHOLE tray of PEAS being spilled all over the floor.

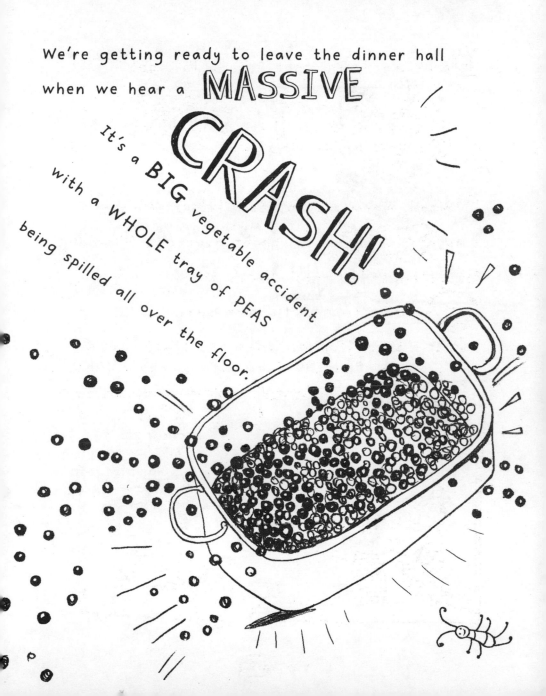

We're trying to see exactly what happened.

Looks like it was that kid Joey (the one who broke my paper banger).

He's accidentally BUMPED into someone who was carrying the peas.

I can hear Caretaker Stan's keys jingling in the distance already, as he dashes to the dinner hall ...

squashed peas

... with a SUPER large BROOM to get the peas under control.

(Which is proving very difficult to do.)

We leave Stan swishing his broom around with a LONG trail of squashed peas behind us.

Mr Fullerman asks everyone to **STAND UP** -

THEN **SIT DOWN** -

then **STAND UP** again and check under their shoes for ←"squashed peas".

(This is another sneaky way of making us practise for SPORTS DAY.)

AMY checks her shoes (which are clean).

Marcus has pea-free shoes as well. But mine are COVERED in peas.

Marcus says it looks like I squashed a frog

and then he makes a big deal of moving his chair right away from me. Mr Fullerman hands me a few paper towels, which get rid of the peas nicely.

Marcus keeps saying YUCK! and pulling horrible faces.

So I tell Marcus that he's got something GREEN stuck between his teeth that doesn't look so good either. He hasn't, but it shuts him up for a bit.

Mr Fullerman wants Marcus to MOVE his chair BACK to where it was. **And stop being so silly.** I agree...

Here's my doodle of Marcus inspired by peas.

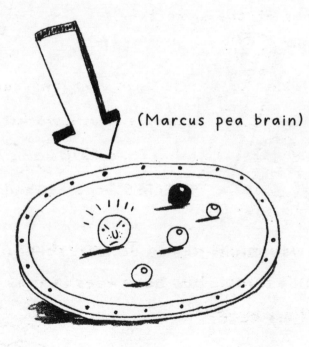

(Marcus pea brain)

ENGLiSh

Eventually we get the **S**quashed peas under control, and **Mr Fullerman** hands out **TWO** WORKSHEETS while making us do some extra arm stretches at the same time.

Stretch up!

He says everyone can choose which worksheet to do. Then he STARES at Brad and says,

"Brad, you might like to do worksheet one? And don't forget, I do have eyes in the back of my head."

Which sounds like an odd thing for **Mr Fullerman** to say.

STOP pulling faces, Brad

Until I read worksheet one. (Brad's been

rumbled.)

Creative Writing Project 1

Read the beginning of this story carefully. Then I'd like YOU to continue the story on a separate piece of paper. Please write at least one A4 page.

It was clear to Mr Fullerman that SOMETHING was going on behind his back. He decided the only thing to do was ...

go home.

The end.

If I were going to write an ending for the story on worksheet one, I'd do this... Ha! Ha!

Bit short, I know. Better do worksheet two instead

if I don't want to get into trouble (again).

Creative Writing Project 2

I would like you to write your own fable with a similar theme to the fable we read in class, "The Boy Who Cried Wolf". The story can be from your own imagination or based on something that might have happened to you in your own life.

At least one A4 page, please.

This is my version of a FABLE – all based on the family barbecue I was telling Derek about earlier that we had last weekend. Enjoy.

The Boy Who Said,

The Sausages Are Burnt

By Tom Gates

This is the story of a family who wouldn't listen to their VERY smart son (that will be me, then). It all began when the SUN came out and my dad thought it would be an EXCELLENT idea to have a barbecue. I said,

Doesn't it always rain when you get out the barbecue, Dad?

And he said,

Don't be daft, of course it's NOT going to rain!

(Like *THAT'S* never happened before.)

So I watched Dad wheel the barbecue out
from the corner of the garden.

It was covered with some special protective plastic that Dad told me would keep it

EXTRA clean and ready to use in an instant!

But underneath the "protective plastic" the barbecue was full of revolting **gunge**.

I told Dad the barbecue didn't look THAT clean? And Dad said that it just needed a quick brush down and all that BLACK **gunge** would BURN off during cooking.

I said,

Are you sure? It looks really disgusting.

But Dad wasn't listening to me. He was looking at Mum, who was *RUNNING* towards us in a very **BIG PANIC**. She told Dad,

I've **COMPLETELY** forgotten that Uncle Kevin and Aunty Alice and the cousins are coming to lunch...

Dad said, When? And Mum said, TODAY... Which would have been OK until she added... In five minutes! Dad said, "Oh great." (But not in a *JOLLY* way.) Mum wanted to know how long the barbecue would take? And I said, "It will take FOREVER, it always does."

But Dad said, Don't listen to Tom.
And gave me a LOOK.
He ASSURED Mum that he knew EXACTLY
what he was doing. "I can just throw on a
couple of extra sausages for them."

Extra
sausages

(Without wanting to SPOIL the story,
you can probably see what's happening here.)

Dad + NOT listening to me ➔ = DISASTER

When Uncle Kevin arrived EARLY,
Dad was busy telling Mum that EVERYTHING
would be fine because he was a

barbecue expert. ☺

And Uncle Kevin said,

HELLO! Did someone say barbecue expert? I'm here!

And Dad whispered, "Great, that's all I need." So Mum suggested that we should leave both the barbecue experts to get on with **burning** the lunch.

Which Dad didn't think was very funny.

All this talk of sausages was making me hungry. I really HOPED the barbecue wasn't going to take too long.

Aunty Alice and the cousins were in the kitchen holding a **MASSIVE** bag of snacks. I told them they should

EAT them NOW

because the barbecue could take **AGES**. Aunty Alice looked **SURPRISED** and said,

You're having a barbecue? I thought it was going to rain.

Mum said it would all be fine. (It wouldn't.) Then she asked me to go up*stairs* and let Delia know that everyone was here. And I said,

What's the point, she won't be pleased to see us.

Which was true.

Mum said, "Just go and knock on her door."

But **I** had a **MUCH** better idea than that.

I showed the cousins how to make some **paper bangers** and how to use them too.

Then we all took them upstairs and stood outside Delia's bedroom door. I think using the paper bangers to let Delia know that everyone was here was a **genius idea!**

Delia came **storming out** of her room and told us to STOP being annoying little boys.

So I told Delia that the cousins were NOT little **and she was being rude.**

Before Delia could get even more grumpy, Mum called upstairs and told us,

The barbecue is nearly ready!

I l👀ked out into the garden but all I could see was

THICK SMOKE EVERYwhere.

The smoke seemed to be getting THiCKeR and thicker. Mum had to rush round the whole house closing the windows to stop the SMOKE from coming in. I couldn't see Dad at all. I could only hear him calling from the smoke-filled garden for someone to...

Bring me a PLATE QUICKLY!

Turns out Uncle Kevin wasn't much help after all. He'd escaped back to the house because he said the smoke was getting in his eyes and he couldn't stop coughing.

coug

cou

Mum handed me a plate 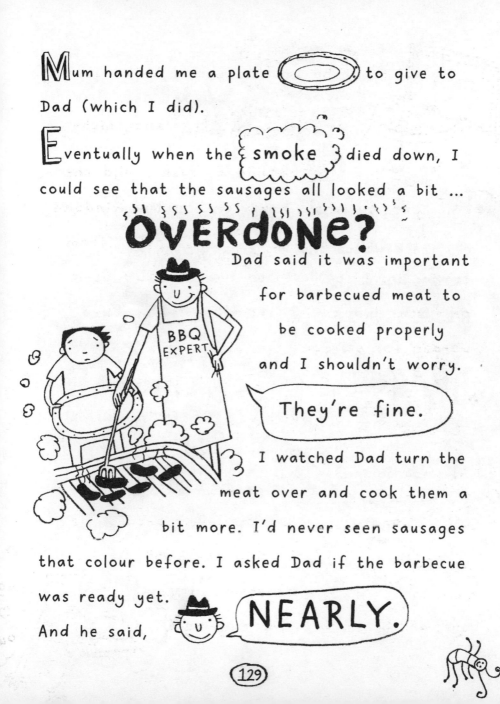 to give to Dad (which I did).

Eventually when the smoke died down, I could see that the sausages all looked a bit ...

OVERDONE?

Dad said it was important for barbecued meat to be cooked properly and I shouldn't worry.

They're fine.

I watched Dad turn the meat over and cook them a bit more. I'd never seen sausages that colour before. I asked Dad if the barbecue was ready yet. And he said, NEARLY.

And I said,

"The sausages look a bit ... **burnt**, Dad?"

And Dad said "They're not burnt, they're just

WELL DONE."

But when he tried to take the sausages

off the barbecue and put them on the plate,

they were ALL

stuck fast

to the nasty black

gunge left on the grill. I reminded

Dad that he said the **gunge** would

burn off
during cooking.   And Dad told me I should go

back to the house and find something more

USEFUL to do.

Tell everyone that lunch is all under control.

(It wasn't.)

I left Dad scraping the sausages up while trying not to make too much of a mess on the plate.

Mum was trying to keep the smoke out of the kitchen with lots of tea-towel wafting. She asked me how everything was going.

I said, OK ... sort of. Which wasn't EXACTLY what Mum wanted to hear.

The cousins had taken my advice and eaten all the snacks. Empty SNacks

BANG

BANG

Now they were playing with their paper bangers again.

I joined in and discovered that if I timed my paper banger SWING just right ...

NOISE

I couldn't hear a word Mum was saying.

"Sorry, Mum?"

BANG!

At least it took my mind off the burnt barbecue lunch that I knew was coming.

FINALLY Dad appeared through the
SWIRLING smoke that was still hanging around

looking very pleased with himself and holding a
nice BIG plate of (**burnt**) barbecued food.
Well, he WAS holding a plate ... right up until I
SWISHED the paper banger over my head and
made a SPECTACULARLY LOUD...

BANG!

And just when Dad thought that this barbecue
couldn't possibly get any worse, it started to
RAIN.

A lot.

Uncle Kevin's eyes got better just in time for him to see all the burnt sausages on the floor.

Dad blamed my paper banger for making him drop the food,

guilty

while the cousins kept asking what was for lunch now?

hungry

Uncle Kevin said,

This is one **BIG** barbecue disaster!

Which was true but <u>not</u> very helpful (and it really annoyed Dad).

I tried to make a suggestion but everyone was distracted by ROOSTER (Derek's dog).

136

Who suddenly JUMPED over the fence and snatched a sausage.

Dad suggested that he could put some more sausages on the barbecue as it was still hot? But Mum wasn't keen on that idea and neither was anyone else. ☹ Especially when the cousins pointed out how many ants were everywhere now.

Then Delia appeared and said,

Where's all the food?

Mum pointed to the ground, then to Rooster. Who was eating → another sausage.

And THAT'S when I managed to

SAVE THE DAY ...

... by suggesting that maybe

we could get a takeaway instead?

TAKE AWAY

Yes, let's!   Yeah   At last   What-ever   Great idea   Lovely

It was the first time ALL day that anyone had really listened to me.

(Better late than never.)
The end.

Result!

There, now that's all done.

I'm about to do some more

when **M**r **F**ullerman
SPOTS what I'm up to.

He announces to the class that if we're
finished, we should

"bring up our books to get them marked

straight away."

I give him my book - and
hope for the best. ☺

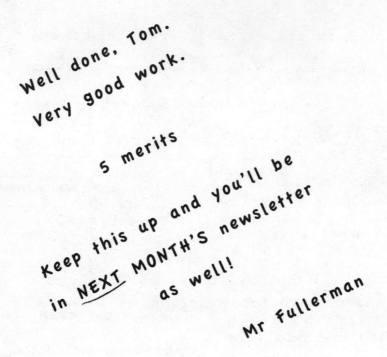

Well done, Tom.
Very good work.

5 merits

Keep this up and you'll be
in NEXT MONTH'S newsletter
as well!

Mr Fullerman

I'd forgotten about my EXCELLENT*
DOODLE book cover being mentioned in the
NEWSLETTER – oh, and with the PHOTO
Mrs Mumble took too.

*See page 357 of Everything's Amazing (Sort Of)
for the whole story.

I'll have to get a few ExTRA copies and leave them lying around the house so Mum and Dad are reminded about my good work and will say nice stuff to me like,

Well done, Tom

while proudly showing off the NEWSLETTER to THE FOSSILS.

Who might even give me some extra pocket money for being such a GOOD hard-working grandson.

You're too kind, Granny.

Then Mum will put the NEWSLETTER on the fridge. (And if she doesn't, I will.) Which will annoy Delia a lot.

I can't wait!

Mr Fullerman says unfortunately this month's NEWSLETTER won't be ready to take home for a few reasons.

Photo-copier

(a few reasons)

Luckily, I have other things to think about as well as my special mention in the NEWSLETTER. Like:

○ Who'll be picked to be a buddy?

Me? Maybe? Maybe not

○ More genius ideas that annoy Delia.

Guess who I am   Very funny

○ The NEW DOGZOMBIES video.

Me, Derek and Norman want to make our very own MUSIC video for DOGZOMBIES (our BAND). We watch DUDE 3 music videos all the

time so thought it would be AMAZING and fun to make our own. We've been talking about it for ages.

Let's do a video

Derek's dad says he can help us. Which is OK as long as he doesn't keep trying to butt in (like usual).

I'm here

He's already been suggesting we watch a few more "classic music videos".

What do you mean you've never seen "Sledgehammer"?

no

no

no

While I'm busy thinking of VIDEO ideas, Mr Fullerman **surprises** me by saying...

"You too, TOM, ARMS UP!"

Because he keeps making us do EXTRA SPORTS DAY practices when we're least expecting it.

Like now.

It's making it VERY difficult to finish off my LARGE doodle. And Marcus keeps on telling Mr Fullerman when I'm drawing. (He's snitched quite a few times now.) Luckily for me, Marcus has been getting on Mr Fullerman's nerves too. He tells Marcus to get on with his own work.

Sir

Which I agree with. 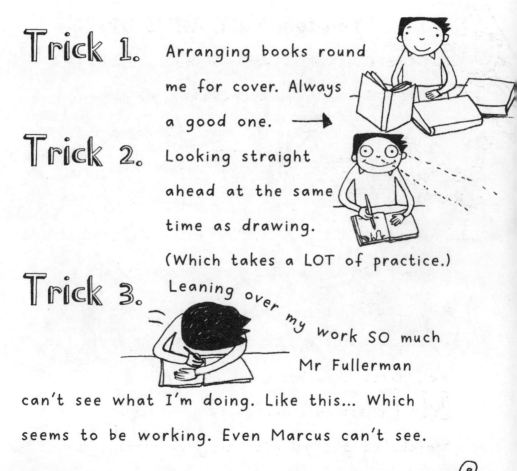 hummph

I've had to use ALL the excellent tricks I know to get this doodle finished.

Trick 1. Arranging books round me for cover. Always a good one. →

Trick 2. Looking straight ahead at the same time as drawing.

(Which takes a LOT of practice.)

Trick 3. Leaning over my work SO much Mr Fullerman can't see what I'm doing. Like this... Which seems to be working. Even Marcus can't see.

(As it's MATHS tomorrow, I'll probably have to start a new one to keep me going.)

BUDDIES

? Today we get to find

out about the buddies...

Oh, and there's maths too. 😕

(Doodle ideas ready if I get bored.)

It's not such a big deal if I don't get chosen.

I tell **AMY** she'll definitely get

picked. And she says, "I'm not so sure."

So I say, "How can you say that?"

And she says, "Who'd pick me?"

I tell **AMY**, "You wouldn't want to pick an

idiot, would you?"

"Thanks, Tom."

Brmmm

Brmmm

It's supposed to be a compliment, but from

the way **AMY** said "Thanks, Tom" maybe it

didn't sound like one.

Mr Fullerman is busy handing out letters about who's going to be a buddy and what they have to do.

Becoming a buddy

Being a buddy to some of the younger
children is a very responsible role.
All buddies are expected to be: helpful,
kind, good listeners with good advice.
Your teachers are there to help.
Remember to be the BEST buddy you
can be!

Mr Keen

He tells the whole class, **"If you don't get chosen this time, you will have another chance next term."**

Then he hands a letter to ...

AMY and I say, "Told you!"

And then to ... ME!

Looks like I'm going to be a buddy to some kid in Class 2R?

Let me see who it is.

Joey Dawson.

That name rings a bell.

Marcus hasn't been chosen this time. He's peering over my shoulder to see who I've got.

He says, "Ha! Ha! That kid is trouble." And I say, "Well, I'm going to be a GOOD buddy and keep him out of trouble."

Then I remember who Joey Dawson is.

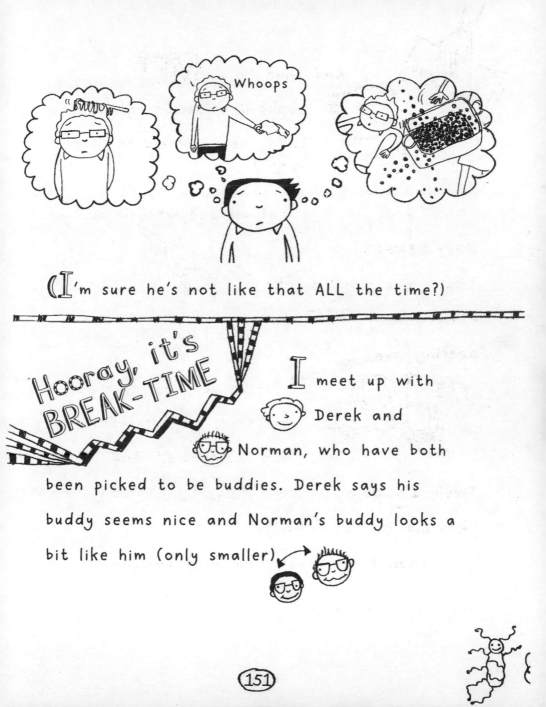

(I'm sure he's not like that ALL the time?)

Hooray, it's BREAK-TIME

I meet up with Derek and Norman, who have both been picked to be buddies. Derek says his buddy seems nice and Norman's buddy looks a bit like him (only smaller)

I can see Joey on the other side of the school grounds. ➡️

He's waving at me. I tell Derek and Norman that he's my buddy.

"Look, here he comes now."

We all watch Joey walk right through a game of football and not notice a thing. Which doesn't go down well with the other kids.

I want to make a good buddy impression, so
I say, "Thanks for choosing me as your buddy, Joey!"

Joey smiles but doesn't say anything.
I'm trying to remember what sort of stuff
is in the letter, and what I'm supposed to be
helping Joey with as his buddy.
I add...
"Got any worries about anything, Joey?"
He shakes his head no.
"Maybe school?"
Joey shakes his head again.
"Friends or teachers giving you a hard time?"
Joey shakes his head.

(This buddy business is going to be easy.)

Then I ask him,

"Have you got any questions you want

to ask me?"

And Joey thinks for a bit ... and says,

"Yes, can I be in your band, please?"

Which takes ALL of us by surprise.

Huh!

I wasn't expecting that question.

So I tell Joey that we're not looking for new

band members right now.

"You can come to our next band practice

and watch us if you want?"

Joey says, "That would be great."

Then he jumps up and down and punches the

air, saying, "YES! YES!" Which is funny!

154

...Until he accidentally

'BIFF'S'

YES

Mr Fullerman, who's walking past him on break
duty. Mr Fullerman is NOT very happy because
he's spilled his cup of tea as well.

He tells Joey, **"Joey, you must be more careful!"**

Then he adds, **"Tom, you're his buddy,**
you should be looking out for him."

Like it was my fault! (It wasn't.)

(155)

Derek and **N**orman think it's a BAD idea to let Joey watch our band practice.

"He'll break something," Derek says.

"He's **worse** than **me**," Norman adds.

The band could definitely do with a practice and **another** gig.

The last time we played, it was for **Granny** Mavis and her Over **70S**

and Make Group.

(Not sure it was a proper gig, though?) I promise Derek and Norman that if Joey turns up, I'll make sure he doesn't touch (or break) anything.

Don't move

(Don't know how ... but I'll try.)

(Granny's Over 70s Cake & Make)

NEWSLETTER

and other interesting facts

Mr Keen, our headmaster (or **RED** master, as I call him when he gets **CROSS**), told us in assembly that the NEWSLETTERS have all been posted to our parents now.

"Along with some other important information AND your mid-term REPORT CARDS!"

I'm hoping that the GOOD mention in the NEWSLETTER will make up for anything dodgy that might be LURKING in my → REPORT CARD. (Fingers crossed there's no mention of made-up LATE NOTES or that kind of thing.)

Mrs Nap goes on to tell everybody about the SCHOOL TALENT-SHOW AUDITIONS. She says we are hoping to see "LOTS OF YOU TALENTED CHILDREN ALL COMING ALONG FOR THE AUDITIONS!"

Mrs Nap explains, "This year's production is a talent show, so anyone can join in. AND there will only be one dress rehearsal once you've been chosen, unlike last year's play."

Which is good to know.

I managed to avoid last year's PLAY - unlike Solid.

(Solid as a tree. He was very good.)

Maybe **DOGZOMBIES** could be part of the show this year, especially with my **NEW GUITAR**, and because **DOGZOMBIES** can now play **SIX** whole songs all the way through.

I can see it now...

Secret MESSAGES (Shhhh)

Back in class,

Mr **F**ullerman has found

yet another way of making

us do EXTRA practice for

SPORTs DAY. We all have to jump up

and touch the arrow before he lets us come

into class. ←

Then he explains to the class what

we'll be doing today.

Top jump
jump

First of all, you need to write the WHOLE alphabet out, and underneath each letter, make up your own symbols. Remember when we looked at the Egyptian hieroglyphics?

That's what I want you all to do.

I thought it sounded a bit dull. Zzzzzzzz yawn yawn... I was getting ready to start a new doodle ... when Mr Fullerman gave us some examples of a SECRET MESSAGE written in code.

We had to work out what the message said. It was BRILLIANT!

Crack the secret code below, then make up your OWN CODE for the alphabet.

Next, we have to invent our OWN CODE.
Which could be VERY useful, especially if I
don't want certain people to know what
I'm writing about...

Marcus is LOOKING

Nosy

? Sniff

at what I'm doing and
SNIFFING right by my ear.
I tell him to stop doing both and he says, "I'm
busy concentrating on my own code" (he's not).
His pen has started to leak and it's

leaving ink on his hands, which

he keeps puting on his face.

I try and tell him what he's doing.
But he ignores me and says

Whatever.

(I did try.)

164

I spend the rest of the lesson making up my own

MONSTER ALIEN

code. Which I am VERY pleased with!

Once we've finished making up our own code, Mr Fullerman wants us to write a letter to the person sitting next to us. I write this one for Marcus, then pass him my ALPHABET so he can work out what it says.

It takes him a while.

Eventually he gets it.

Ha! Ha!

Joey

Buddy duties are proving to be trickier than I first thought. Every SINGLE break-time and lunchtime, Joey comes to say

Hello!

But that's ALL he says. (Joey doesn't talk much.) I tried to pass a few tips on about getting by in Oakfield School.

But it's hard to tell if he's interested or not.

Mr Fullerman is on break duty (again) and he's looking over in my direction. So I'm trying to show him that I'm being an excellent buddy.

I ask Joey if he'd like to have a game of
football with me and a few of my friends,

"Just a little kick around."
And Joey nods YES.

So I get a ⚽ ball and ask Derek
and Solid to join in too. We're

kicking it ⚽ to each other, nothing fancy.

Joey's actually pretty good at football. He's doing
OK. **Mr Fullerman** is still wandering around the
school grounds keeping an eye on everyone. And
(hopefully) noticing what a GOOD buddy I'm being.
I kick the football HIGH in the air and call out,

"Joey ... on your head!" And Joey jumps up
and tries to HEAD the ball back to me...

Well, I think that's what he wanted to do.

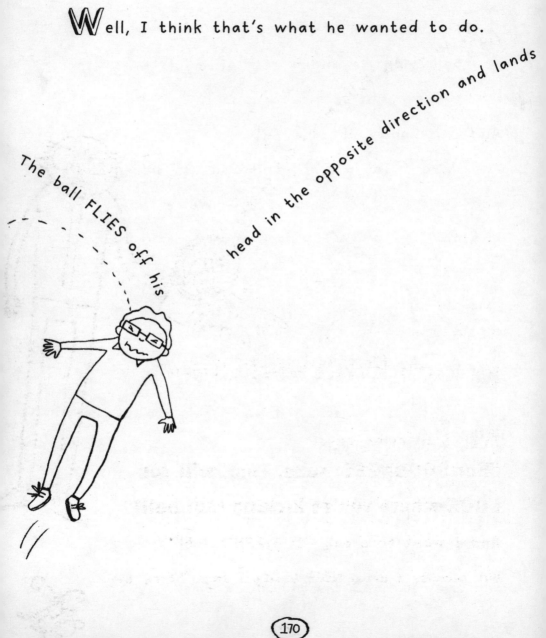

head in the opposite direction and lands

The ball FLIES off his

right in ... Mr Fullerman's cup of tea.

Which spills EVERYWHERE (again).

Mr Fullerman says,
**"For GOODNESS' sake, Tom, will you
LOOK where you're kicking that ball!"**

And I want to shout, "It WASN'T ME!"

But because I am a NICE buddy, I say..."Sorry, sir."

Marcus has been watching us and comes over.

Joey ←

He says, "I'm glad I don't have a buddy like yours."

And I say, "It was an accident, wasn't it, Joey?"

But Joey's already gone back into school to avoid Mr Fullerman and me (I think).

Marcus says, "I told you your buddy was trouble."

Thanks for that, Marcus.

On the way home from school, Derek gets out TWO caramel wafers.

"My buddy gave them to me for being nice." And I'm thinking I DESERVE LOADS of WAFERS for not snitching on Joey. (Who's been staying out of my way since the football incident.)

Derek gives me one of his wafers, which is nice of him. I try and make mine last all the way home by eating it in sections.

Like this

Break in half

Eat in sections

I'm just finishing the last tiny little bit when I open the front door, go into the kitchen and find THIS PINNED UP ON THE FRIDGE!

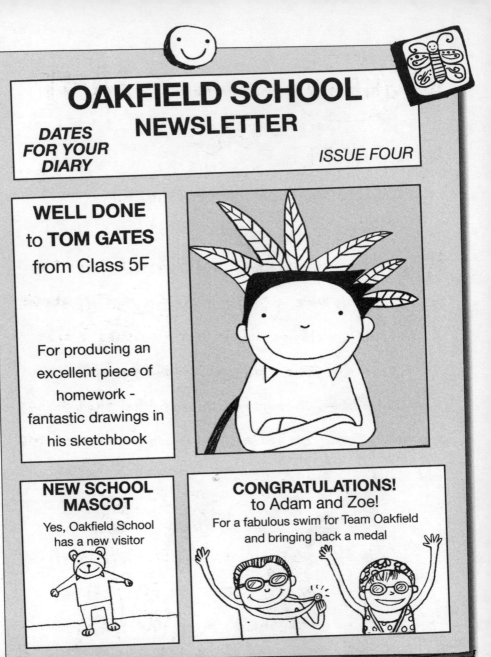

OAKFIELD SCHOOL
NEWSLETTER

DATES FOR YOUR DIARY

ISSUE FOUR

WELL DONE to **TOM GATES** from Class 5F

For producing an excellent piece of homework - fantastic drawings in his sketchbook

NEW SCHOOL MASCOT

Yes, Oakfield School has a new visitor

CONGRATULATIONS!
to Adam and Zoe!
For a fabulous swim for Team Oakfield and bringing back a medal

My (HEAD) looks like a GIANT

PINEAPPLE.

(Shame.)

Mum says she is VERY pleased with me. But we need to have a little (CHAT) about a few other things when Dad finishes work.

(We do? That doesn't sound good.)

The only time Mum says things like that is if I'm in trouble or if Delia has been blaming ME for stuff I didn't do.

Who ate all the jam?

Empty

Tom did

Who used all the towels?

Tom did

Delia is upstairs LURKING around in the bathroom. I'm going to ask her what she's been saying about me NOW?

I wait for Delia to come out ...

... and when she does, I notice that her hair has turned a VERY odd colour.
It looks a bit ... green?

It IS GREEN!

I follow Delia into her room to get a PROPER look.

But she shuts the door and tells me to

GET LOST!

I ask her through the closed door, "What happened to your hair, Delia?"

And she tells me to

"Go AWAY, you're annoying."

So I say, "Did you know your hair's GREEN?"

Followed by,

"Why the GREEN hair?"

Delia says if I don't go away she'll tell Mum that I've been writing my own LATE NOTES

How does she know that?

I go back to my room and while I'm thinking of excuses in case Mum and Dad ask me about my late note ... I have a

GENIUS IDEA

for a song.

Which goes like this...
(As I've written down the words, it seems a shame not to do some nice drawings to go with it?)

GREEN

AGH!

Delia ... doesn't want to be SEEN

Because her hair has gone bright GREEN.

It looks the colour of a LEAF

Now Mum and Dad will give her GRIEF.

She tried to make her hair look FINE

But now it's gone a shade of LIME.

Delia ... she can be MEAN.
Delia ... her hair is GREEN.

GREEN

I go back downstairs (still singing my new song) and Mum wants to know what I'm singing about.

Delia's GREEN hair.

Delia's clean hair?

And I say, No, green hair.

Then Dad comes in from his shed and CONGRATULATES me on being in the NEWSLETTER, then adds that we need to talk about a few other things too.

So I change the subject quickly and say, "Delia's got green hair."

Just then, THE FOSSILS (Granny Mavis and Granddad Bob) 'POP' in to say "hello". Like they do. And Granny says, "Who's got GREEN hair?"

Hello

Hello

And I say, "Delia."

Granddad laughs and says, "At least she's got hair, not like me!"

Then I add, Or Dad. Which is true, but Dad doesn't look too happy now.

Mum goes upstairs to see Delia, and Dad says he's off to get changed.

Granny Mavis mentions she's taken up knitting again. She says, "I could make Delia a **HAT** if she needs one?"

Which is a GREAT idea.

May be I should help Granny with a few hat ideas.

Like these...

(This one is my personal favourite.)

Dad suddenly appears wearing → THOSE shorts again.

He tells everyone "I'm going for a brisk run," (like we wanted to know),

Then Mum comes back downstairs and says that Delia's had a bit of a

HAIR-DYE DISASTER.

I say, "Really? I hadn't noticed." Mum says, "She's probably been using some TERRIBLE cheap hair dye. Not like the one I use."

I tell Mum that Granny Mavis has offered to knit Delia a hat.

"To cover up her green HAIR."

Mum says,

Actually, Delia's quite upset about her hair and doesn't want to see anyone because she's feeling a bit...

And I say, Like a tree?

Mum gives me a look and says,

No, Tom, she's feeling a bit self-conscious and embarrassed.

Granny says "Poor Delia" then tells us they're off to the shops to pick up a few odds and ends.

(From the look of Granny's list, it's mostly "odd" things.)

Buy ingredients for
sausage and jam rolls

peach and pea soup

Raspberry & tomato PIE

Then Mum says BYE to **THE FOSSILS** who wish her **LUCK** sorting everything out.

Mum WAS being all nice and sympathetic about Delia's hair.

Poor Delia

Right up until she discovered it was **HER** hair dye Delia had been using. Now she's really **NOT** happy about that!

FAB HAIR DYE

It's quite late when Dad gets back from his run. He looks **RED** in the face and is limping a bit. He says,

Puff
Puff

"I'm in agony, I think I've pulled a muscle."

Mum asks, "Is that part of your carefully planned fitness regime too?"

Then she says, "At least you have an excuse not to run in the PARENTS' RACE on Tom's SPORTS DAY."

How did she know about my SPORTS DAY? I've been keeping it quiet. Especially after last year's race.

Dad

Mr Fingle

(Last year's race)

I say, "You don't HAVE to come, my class are always **LAST** anyway."

Dad says he'll be **fine** and he's looking forward to running and **BEATING** Derek's dad this time. (I'm not.)

Mum wants to know if I'm auditioning for the school talent show tomorrow as well?

How does she know about that?

"I read your **NEWSLETTER** and your mid-term→ REPORT CARD too."

Oh! Oh! My report card has arrived.

Dad says, Which reminds me, we want to talk to you about your report card, Tom.

(I'm getting worried now.)

$\mathbb{D}$ad limps over to get it. I can't remember anything **BAD** that I've done (apart from the LATE NOTE and a few other notes too).

Mum and Dad are both looking at me with very serious faces. They say, "**Tom**, we are very surprised that..."

You are an idiot

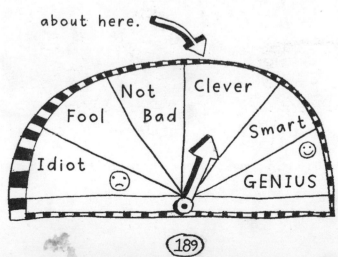

"You're doing SO WELL! It's amazing. Well done! Keep it UP!"

WOW! That's a first for me. My report card usually says things like:

Tom does too much chatting/doodling.

Tom doesn't do enough homework/

maths.

But now on a scale of Idiot to Genius I'm about here.

Fool   Not   Clever
       Bad
                Smart
Idiot
       ☹   ☺
              GENIUS

Mum thinks I should put my guitar to good use and enter **DOGZOMBIES** in the talent show. "You're doing so well at everything!"

Good point. Maybe we could do it?

I give Norman a ring first and then Derek to see if they agree.

Let's!

Yeah

They do.

While I'm on the phone to Derek, I remind him about last year's parents' race and how embarrassing it was watching our dads run.

Then I have a **Terrible** thought. "Cycling shorts ... my dad could turn up wearing those cycling shorts!"

Derek says,

Shame.

While we're chatting on the phone, I can hear Rooster in Derek's garden running around **barking** like MAD. Derek says Rooster's been chewing all his socks, which is driving him **BONKERS**. And I suddenly think of an excellent way to avoid a possible SPORTS DAY cycling shorts shame after all.

(Genius idea. 💡)

SPORTS DAY!

Now Dad's cycling shorts have miraculously disappeared, I'm fine with him and Mum both coming to my SPORTS DAY.

    I'd better remember to bring ALL my own sports kit (for good reason). On the way to school, Derek tells me that his dad has actually been

Wear this

practising for the parents' race.

He has? Wow, that's embarrassing.

Before we go to the sports ground, Mr Fullerman gives the whole class what he calls a

motivational talk.

His eyes look even **bigger** than usual because he is all enthusiastic.

GO FOR IT, CLASS 5F! TRY YOUR BEST AND HAVE FUN.

I say to **AMY**,

"**W**hat he really means is ... don't be rubbish and come last again."

Which is true.

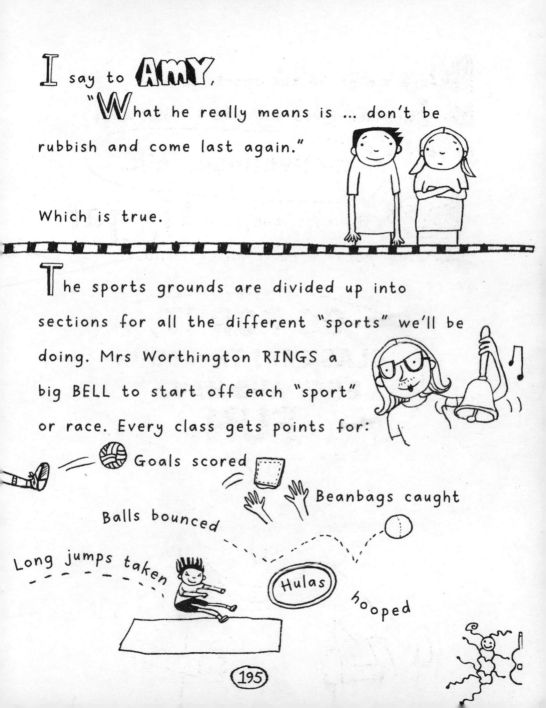

The sports grounds are divided up into sections for all the different "sports" we'll be doing. Mrs Worthington RINGS a big BELL to start off each "sport" or race. Every class gets points for:

Goals scored

Beanbags caught

Balls bounced

Long jumps taken

Hulas hooped

When all the classes have done every "sport", ☆ the points are added up and the **WINNERS** are announced – after the parents' race, of course.

Mr Sprocket's class are wearing vests with **SLOGANS** on so they look like a proper team.

We just look like ... Class 5F.
Mrs Worthington rings the bell)) to begin the first session.

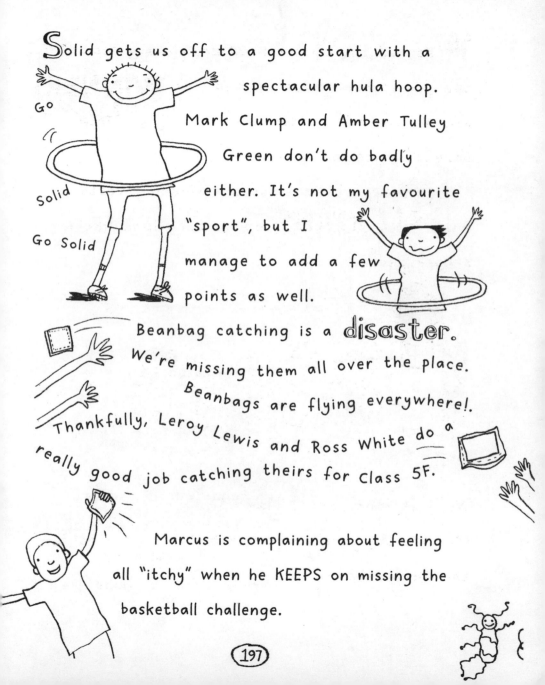

Solid gets us off to a good start with a spectacular hula hoop. Mark Clump and Amber Tulley Green don't do badly either. It's not my favourite "sport", but I manage to add a few points as well.

Go

Solid

Go Solid

Beanbag catching is a disaster. We're missing them all over the place. Beanbags are flying everywhere!. Thankfully, Leroy Lewis and Ross White do a really good job catching theirs for Class 5F.

Marcus is complaining about feeling all "itchy" when he KEEPS on missing the basketball challenge.

197

And he blames me for *shoving* him, which I did (accidentally).

Mr Fullerman seems to be smiling, which is better than last year.

Oh well

AMY and Indrani are telling Julia that she's doing really well and not to be nervous about the long jump, which is our last sport.

It's not helping that Mr Sprocket is leading his class in a LOUD...

Give me a **W**

Give me an **I**

Give me an **N**

Give me another **N**

Give me an **E**

Give me an **R**

Give me an **S**

What have you got?

There's a slight pause as none of the class can work out what they've just spelled. In the end it's Mr Fullerman who says...

"It spells WINNERS, but don't count on it"

to Mr Sprocket's class.

Mr Fullerman's 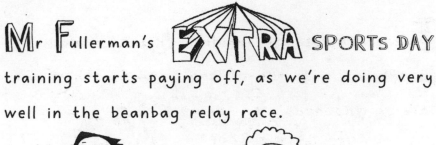 SPORTS DAY training starts paying off, as we're doing very well in the beanbag relay race.

Mr Keen is wandering around saying

encouraging things like:

"Perfect pass, Pansy" and

"Really fast run, Robert."

There are lots of families, friends and parents on one side of the grounds behind a barrier who are *cheering* too.

I can't see 👁 👁 anyone from my family ... yet. Mrs Worthington rings the bell for everyone to stop for:

Drinks, oranges and BISCUITS.

Which is VERY popular. During the break, Mr Fullerman tells us that everyone is doing BRILLIANTLY and we're definitely NOT going to come last this year.

Yes! Yes!

(I think he's more pleased than we are.)

Norman has somehow managed to eat **WAY** too many biscuits. And as the sugar starts to **kick** in, he's rolling around on the ground with his legs in the *air* saying...

Look, I'm a dying fly!

"Yes, you are, Norman."

(Oh dear.)

The last sport for Class 5F is the **long** jump. I still can't see any of my family in the crowd at **all**. Until **AMY** says,

You're popular.

I glance over to where Amy's looking.

Now I can see ...

... AND HEAR them.

(Shame.)

I manage to get THE FOSSILS not to wave the

WE LOVE YOU, TOM banner.

Luckily, I'm not the only one with an embarrassing family. Julia Morton's parents are wearing T-shirts ...

with her FACE on them.

JuLia STAR!

Julia STAR!

Which hasn't helped her feel any less NERVOUS.

Oh NO!

Mrs Worthington rings the bell and says, "It's time for the last sport. GOOD luck!"

Which is **LONG** JUMP in our case.
I take my turn ... *run* as
fast as I can and ...

...throw myself into the sand pit.

Yes

It's not a bad j u m p either.
Good enough for **THE FOSSILS** to take out

the **WE LOVE YOU, TOM** banner again.

Yeah

Most of the class have jumped and there's just TWO kids to go.
Mr Fullerman (who's been having a sneaky peek ◯ ◯ at the scores) says,

Only a few points between
Mr Sprocket's class and us now.

Which is good news.

The last TWO jumps need to be as
LONG as POSSIBLE!

Julia Morton and Marcus say

OK

But I'm not sure they're
feeling confident.

Marcus goes first. The class start clapping
to help him jump further. When he starts
running, they all say...

"Whhhhhooooooooooooooooo!"

until he lands.

Then it's an, "Oooooooh?" as his long jump is ... only a tiny bit better than last time.

Itchy →

Marcus says he got distracted in mid-air by his **ITCHY** T-shirt. (If you say so, Marcus.)

Then Julia goes to jump.

She looks very **NERVOUS**.

The class go...

Whhhhhoooo

oooo!

Because Julia's jump is AMAZING!
We're all cheering and clapping. But we won't
know who's won the SPORTS DAY trophy
until after the parents' races.
(I'd forgotten about that)

Just like last year, some dads are taking the race a LOT more seriously than others. My dad is trying to pretend the race is

Just a bit of FUN.

But from the Determined LOOK on his face and the fancy running shoes he's wearing, I can tell he wants to WIN.

Mrs Worthington sets them off with a whistle this time.

Fancy trainers

Dad manages to HUFF and PUFF himself into ...

THIRD PLACE!

(Embarrassing headband)

PUFF

YES!

Ahead of Derek's dad (Mr Fingle), which he is VERY pleased about.

I say to Derek, "Phew, over for another year!" And Derek says, "I can't believe my dad wore that headband."

(I'm guessing Rooster might have something else to play with later.)

Mum says she can't run in the "mums' race" because she's worn the wrong shoes (accidentally on purpose, I think).

whoops!

Now the **THE FOSSILS** want to know why there isn't a grandparents' race too? (I'm sort of glad there isn't, to be honest.)

Mr Keen comes over and says they have added up ALL the points and are ready to announce the

"winner of this year's SPORTS DAY Trophy, who is ...

Class 5N!"

It's Mrs Nap's class ... and we're SECOND. In front of Mr Sprocket's class. But from the way Mr Fullerman is leaping around and

Cheering

you'd think it was us who had won.

I've never seen him so happy.

The VERY best thing about coming second at SPORTS DAY is that Mr Fullerman is in an EXCELLENT mood 😊 for the rest of the week.

He has made a special SPORTS DAY

DISPLAY, which is ...

SECOND 5F THIRD 5S

SECOND WERE CLASS 5F

Sports Day was won this year by 5N

Everyone who took part had a fantastic time. Especially 5F and Mr Fullerman.

... right outside Mr Sprocket's classroom.

**Sports Day
Winners 5N**

The morning of the auditions for the school **Talent Show**

I'm a bit achy after SPORTS DAY. (All that jumping into sandpits and catching beanbags.)

On the way to school Derek and I discuss the audition and what song we should play. Derek says it has to be "Smoke on the Water".

And I say, Why's that?

And Derek says, "Because the old folks loved that song and Mrs Nap and Mr Sprocket are quite old so they'll like it too."

218

Good point. ⇨

"Smoke on the Water"

Old folks enjoying the song

I've brought my new guitar to school. And I'm
a bit nervous that something might happen to
it. I get even more worried when the first
person we see is ...

Joey.

He's not been around much
since the football incident.
But because I am a GOOD buddy,
I say, Hi, Joey and tell him
we're auditioning for the school talent show.
He says, I'll see you there.

He will?

Straight away I'm thinking, I'll have to keep
an EXTRA eye on my guitar. I don't want
anything happening to it with Joey around.

In class, I ask Mr Fullerman if he could keep his beady eyes 👀 on my guitar until it's time for the auditions. I don't ask him like THAT.
Obviously.

Please, Mr Fullerman, could you keep my guitar in a safe place?

AMY, Indrani and Florence are all singing for their audition. I ask Marcus what he's doing and he says,

"A magic act that I've been practising a LOT. So it's really good."

And I say, Can you do any magic now?

And he says no because he needs his special box of magic tricks. Which sounds interesting.

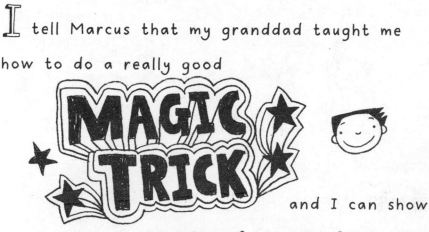

I tell Marcus that my granddad taught me how to do a really good

MAGIC TRICK

and I can show him if he wants?

Marcus says,

"Go on, then ... impress me."

MY GRANDDAD'S MAGIC TRICK

Empty

Granddad's trick goes like this...

1. Take a tissue and **scrunch** it up in your hand, then say

> I can make it **disappear.**

2. Then stand up and hold the tissue in your hand. Move your hand up and down while counting to four like this.

One...

Two...

Three...

Four...

3. Then on the fourth or fifth time, LET GO of the tissue by throwing it $\boxed{\text{behind}}$ the person's head so they don't see it.

Now open your hand really slowly to show that the tissue has DISAPPEARED.

It does take a bit of practice.

Gone

But it worked really well on Marcus.

School Talent Show AUDITIONS

Joey comes to our classroom to collect us for our audition because he is helping Mr Sprocket.

I hold on to my guitar tightly and say, "Hi, Joey." He nods hello.

Ready?

We're walking to the hall when Norman says, " are definitely coming to play here because the whole school are talking about it."

And I say, "I hope it's **TRUE**, Norman. It would be **SO** good."

(Rumours often start in school that aren't true.)

Rumour in school

Frisbee →

What really happened

Derek is already waiting for us along with Marcus (who's auditioning next).

Marcus is wearing ... a **CAPE.**

He's swishing it around and trying to be all dramatic.

Mr Sprocket calls out,

DOGZOMBIES NEXT, PLEASE.

But before we can start, Mr Sprocket asks for help

carrying some chairs and checking the drum kit is at the right height first, please.

We have no choice.

Just prop your guitar over there for a second, Tom.

I'm NOT going to do THAT! So Joey offers to

hold it. And I have to stop myself from saying,

NO WAY!

Then MARCUS says, I'll look after it.

Which is only a tiny bit better than Joey, but

I don't have much of a choice. So while we go

with Mr Sprocket to pick up the chairs and a

few music stands, Marcus is left

holding my guitar. Like this... ➡

I can see 👀 him FIDDLING with the

strings! I tell him, "Don't touch the strings."

But he ignores me. Now he's TWIDDLING with

the end of my guitar and doing ROCK STAR

poses while pretending to play it. I can't

take my guitar

back FAST enough!

Marcus says, "Don't snatch."
Guitar in hand – we get ready for our audition.

Hello – we're **DOGZOMBIES**.

But when I start to play "SMOKE ON THE WATER", it doesn't sound like "Smoke on the Water". It sounds **TERRIBLE**.

My guitar has gone out of tune because Marcus was fiddling **SO MUCH** with the strings. I have to keep going.

But it's a rotten audition. I can tell from the faces Mr Sprocket and Mrs Nap are pulling. They look like they're in pain.

When we've finished, Mr Sprocket says,

> Well done. Just a few tuning issues to be sorted out ... but not bad, boys.

Which is better than I thought. Derek tells me not to worry. Norman says,

> It wasn't so bad.

Marcus says, "What happened? You lot were RUBBISH! More like DOG'S DINNER than DOGZOMBIES."

Which is irritating ... but true. Derek says, "Thanks, Marcus. Let's see how YOU do, then?" Marcus SWISHES his cape and goes off to perform.

He announces himself as ✦ "MAGIC ✦ MARCUS".

Which sounds like MAGIC MARKERS and makes us all LAUGH. Ha! Ha! Ha!

Marcus is doing tricks with cards and all kinds of different things and is surprisingly good, which is a bit annoying.

Now Joey has brought along AMY, Florence and Indrani for their audition.

"How did you do?" Amy asks me.

I was about to say, "Not bad ... or OK, but might have done better" when Joey decides to BUTT in and tells AMY,

They were TERRIBLE, all out of tune.

Thanks, Joey! He's normally quiet. Some buddy he turned out to be. It wasn't my fault the guitar went out of tune.

I tell Derek and Norman that "Marcus will probably go around telling EVERYONE how BAD DOGZOMBIES were."

And Derek says, Do you think so?

Yes, that's EXACTLY what Marcus does.

Hopeless, they were

Shame

DOGZOMBIES were RUBBISH

Oh dear

It was painful to listen to

Now ALL the School are talking about DUDE3 playing at the school talent show. AND the RUBBISH audition DOGZOMBIES did.

Which was THE WORST audition EVER in the WHOLE HISTORY of the school.

(That last bit's not true ... but that's what it FEELS like everyone is saying.)

It's not very long before the list of successful AUDITIONS gets pinned up on the school notice board. Somehow ... DOGZOMBIES has made it.

Oakfield School Talent Show Audition Results

If your name is below, you're in the SHOW!
We'll have ONE dress rehearsal before the show.
Well done, EVERYONE

Brad Galloway

Julia Morton

Minnie Verner

June Rawlings

Tom Gates

Norman Watson

Derek Fingle

Marcus Meldrew

Amy Porter

Indrani Hindle

Florence Mitchell

Paul Rogers

Jenny Chan

Christina Brown

Roger Wood

Emily Border

Chad Dury

Paul Jolly

SPECIAL GUEST APPEARANCE TO BE ANNOUNCED

In fact, looking at the list, I think **everyone** who auditioned made it.

Right at the bottom it says

SPECIAL GUEST APPEARANCE

to be announced.

Which looks interesting?

Could the RUMOURS be true after all?

Family Outing to the CINEMA

On the way home we BUMP into Joey going the other way.

(When I say we bumped into him ... I mean we BUMPED into him.)

I ask him if he's OK?

He nods. Then he says,

When can I come to your band practice?

I'd forgotten about that.

And I'm looking at Derek, who seems a bit alarmed.

AGh!

DOG Zombie

236

I tell Joey that we're SUPPOSED to be filming our BAND [VIDEO] soon.

It might not be a good time to come and watch us. Sorry.

Joey says, I could come and help you and bring WAFERS.

And Derek shrugs his shoulders like it's OK with him. So I say, "OK, Joey, it'll be at Derek's house. I'll let you know when."

Joey says, "Yeah, thanks." Then he runs off and bumps into someone else coming around the corner.

AGH! Whoops

When I get home Mum reminds me that we're supposed to be having some

QUALITY family time together tonight.

And I say, We are?

"Yes, we're going to the cinema. We have to go somewhere dark or Delia won't come with us while her hair's still a bit GREEN."

"What are we seeing?"

Mum says it's a great film that's had lots of good reviews.

"It's called The Otter."

And I say, What's it about? Because I've never heard of the film? Then Delia butts in and she says,

It's about an OTTER, stupid.

So I say, "Not necessarily, it could be a film about SPIES and 'THE OTTER' is a code name for a secret agent."

And Delia says,

"OR it could be about an OTTER and that's why there's a MASSIVE picture on the film poster of AN OTTER."

The OTTER

Mum says, "All right, Delia, that's enough."

Then I suggest that if Delia doesn't want to be seen with her :**GREEN**: hair, she could always ask Granny Mavis to knit one of these hats for her?

Like this or this.

Then Dad comes in and says,

Has anyone seen my cycling shorts? I can't find them any where.

This seems like a good time to disappear to my room and wait until we're all ready to go.

W hich takes AGES.

WAIT! I forgot my glasses

W e're so late we nearly miss the start of

the film. As we're buying the tickets, Mum

is getting STRESSED because she likes

to sit near the ——▶ FRONT of the cinema

and she's worried it will all be FULL.

And she HATES it when people eat too

LOUDLY. Mum thinks there should be

RULES for what you

can eat in the

cinema.

Crunch

Munch

Slurp

I've brought a few fruit chews that I unwrap BEFORE the film starts. Otherwise Mum will keep STARING and nudging me until I stop.

We all manage to get seats near the front before the film starts. Delia has got her hood up and looks even more grumpy than usual. I tell Dad that I don't want to sit next to her if she's taking off her sunglasses again.

Grump
→

So Dad sits between us.

We're all settled and the lights are just going down. Mum's happy with her seat. There's no one eating too LOUDLY near us. Everything is great. When this happens to me...

I can't see a thing now!

That's just great. I keep moving from side to side but I still can't see the film. Mum tells me to stop fidgeting, Tom.

SWAPPED

I say, "I can't see." So Mum swaps seats with me. And for about a minute I can see the whole screen.

Then the TALLEST man in the world with the ← BIGGEST head does this ... and that's when I realize who's sitting in front of me.

It's Solid and HIS DAD.

I tap him on the back and say, "Hi!" And Mum says, "Shhhhhh."

I decide to go and sit next to him because I can't see anything behind him or his dad.

The film is REALLY Funny. Even Delia is laughing (but I'm not going to look at her without her glasses again).

Mum keeps tapping me on the head every time Solid and I chat. Even a tiny bit.

Solid says, "Are your whole family here?"

And I whisper,

 "Yes, we're having quality family time watching a film. So we don't have to talk to each other."

Then Mum Taps me on the head again and tells me to...

 Shhhhhhhhh...

Groan

When the film is finished, Dad says he's going to the toilet and he'll meet us outside. We all get up to leave and Solid and I are **chatting** about the film, our SPORTS DAY and the school auditions, STUFF like that.

It's only when he says (BYE) and walks off with his dad that I realize how similar they both are.

Solid   His dad

Mum wants to know what's taking Dad so long and she goes off to find him, leaving me outside with Delia (who's getting grumpier).

Then suddenly Delia notices that Ed, her old boyfriend, is coming out of the cinema with some of his friends. She tells me, "Don't move or ELSE." And ducks behind me.

I decide to have some fun and start moving from side to side so Delia has to follow me. I can hear Delia whispering behind me, "Don't you DARE" as Ed looks up and sees me. I wave and say, "Hi, Ed, fancy seeing you here."

Ed comes over and says, "Hi, Tom." And I say, "Good film, wasn't it?" and he says, "Great ... are you still in your band?"

And I say, "Yes, thanks."

Delia's still crouched down with her hood covering her GREEN hair and she's trying to sneak away without Ed noticing. Which might have worked if I hadn't moved out of the way at exactly the same time as a

BIG gust of wind SWEEPS Delia's hood right off her head. Delia's GREEN hair stands out a LOT.

Wow!
Green
hair

Surprise!

Everyone is looking at her - including Ed.

Mum and Dad come back just in time to

stop Delia from taking her **REVENGE**

on me. She says, "You wait."

Which doesn't sound good.

So I suggest Delia lightens up

and has some FUN. "Like me!"

Mum says it's nice that we're

both enjoying ourselves.

(Well, I am... Delia looks a bit grumpy and

GREEN. still.)

Missing **Homework**

With all the stuff that's been going on in school, it's easy to forget about my...

Homework?

Because **M**r **F**ullerman is STILL in a super good mood from SPORTS DAY, he says I can bring it in tomorrow. Which is good news for me.

I've been spending **LOADS** of my time at home (and in class) PLANNING and thinking of ideas for the DOGZOMBIES VIDEO.

Planning for the video

WILD Thing | Video M M

There are SO many things we could do. Like:
○ Make **WILD THING** masks.

WILD THING

○ Make **WILD THING** posters to put in the background.

○ Film in the garden, which looks a bit jungley in parts.

I've got LOADS of IDEAS going on in my head. And writing a WHOLE A4 page about "MY SPORTS DAY" just isn't one of them.

"Tomorrow" has come round a bit **too** quickly - I've only managed to write a bit of my homework while on the way to school this morning.

I have to finish it off under my desk ... and on my lap ... so **M**r **F**ullerman can't see what I'm doing.

Under the circumstances I think I've done OK?

My Sports Day

By TOM GATES

I REALLY LIKED SPORTS DAY THIS YEAR BECAUSE WE NEARLY WON! YEAH! AND MR FULLERMAN HAS BEEN IN A GOOD MOOD.

WE HAD NICE ORANGE BISCUITS, WHICH WAS A TREAT. YEAH!

Tom ....

Y o u   s   e   e   m

t   o   b   e

s   p   a   c   i   n   g

o   u   t   your words a lot?

This does not fool me into thinking
you have done a whole A4 page!

Don't try this again.

Mr Fullerman

Phew ... could have been worse.

No detention or mention of "EXTRA WORK".

DOGZOMBIES VIDEO

After an **EXHAUSTING** week at school, me, Norman and Derek are very busy making some important decisions about the **DOGZOMBIES** video that we're filming today.

1. Hats or no hats?

2. Sunglasses or no sunglasses?

3. Outside or inside?

4. Masks or no masks?

5. Wafers now or later? Cool!

Wafers later is the only decision we've made so far. Mostly because we don't want Norman to peak too soon.

I say, "What do you think **DUDE3** would do if they were making this **video?**" Derek says he doesn't think they'd wear masks.

It's a good point. We stick to the **DOGZOMBIES** T-shirts instead and film inside Derek's garage, as it looks like it might rain. Mr Fingle 😊 has offered to help out and has set up the camera on his fancy TRIpod. Which is great. But it does mean we can't move around much or we won't be in shot.

Derek's dad starts talking about classic music videos of our time.

AGAIN.

So Derek has to remind him that we're just doing this for fun. We're saved when Mr Fingle's phone rings – which keeps him busy for a bit. Derek says, "Shall we just press play on the camera and have a go then?"

It's a good plan. But we can't work out who's going to do it, because it's tricky pressing play, then running back into shot. We're just about to start filming when this time MRS Fingle comes in! She says, "You have a visitor to see DOGZOMBIES!" We do?

Hello It's Joey.

Who I invited round to watch us do a band practice ... and then forgot all about.

Come round tomorrow

Ok

Joey says his mum will be picking him up in two hours.

And Derek says,

"TWO HOURS!"

like it's a really really long time. Then Joey shows us a very small cool camera that his mum has lent him to use today. "I can do some filming too if you want?"

Which is an **excellent** idea.

(Joey's turning out to be really helpful after all.)

Though Joey does *knock* the tripod over twice.

whoops

Mr Fingle comes back and starts making a few filming suggestions.

Some are better than others...

Stand on one leg ... then PLAY!

Really?

But it does make TWO HOURS WHIZZ by.

J oey's mum turns up just as we're really getting into filming. She says, "This looks good! I'll help you put the video together if you want."

Joey's mum →

Norman says, "**SWEET**."

(He means that's good.)

Then Joey says, "That reminds me - I brought you these."

He throws me a whole pack of

caramel WAFERs!

YEAH! Then knocks over the camera for the THIRD time.

Mr Fingle's checking his camera's still working (it is). I'm thinking Joey has turned out to be an excellent buddy after all.

TALENT SHOW → rehearsal

Mr Fullerman

reminds us that there's a

"RUN-THROUGH today for the school talent show before the REAL show, which is ... tonight."

I whisper to **AMY,** *Tonight! Is he sure?*

And Mr Fullerman says, **"Yes, Tom, tonight."**

How could I have forgotten when the school production was?

TALENT SHOW is THIS THURSDAY. DON'T FORGET!

SCHOOL NOTICE BOARD

TALENT

TALENT SHOW TONIGHT Special Guests

The GOOD news is **DOGZOMBIES**
rehearsal time is at 11:15. It looks like I'll be
missing ... MATHS. ☺
Result! (Making the **DOGZOMBIES** video
was a bit of extra practice for us too, which
is good.)

Marcus has his run-through before
us at eleven o'clock. He's sitting next to me
complaining (as usual). He thinks he should be
on last. And I say, "How do you work
that one out, Marcus?" and he says,
"Because my act is the best one." And
I say, "It might not be?"

And he says, "No one else is doing
magic tricks like me."

And I say, "What about the

SPECIAL GUESTS?

There's a RUMOUR that DUDE 3 are coming to our school. They're better than you."

 And he says, "Don't be STUPID ... DUDE 3 won't come to our school. That's not going to happen, is it?"

Then he starts SCRATCHING his back, which makes ME feel itchy too. I stop scratching when I notice AMY, Indrani and Florence are looking at me.

They are getting ready to sing after **DOGZOMBIES**, followed by Mark Clump.

Who apparently is bringing in one of his **pets** that he's trained to do tricks.

(Maybe his snake? Which would be impressive.) Brad is doing street dancing (not behind **M**r **F**ullerman's back this time either).

I *wish* I knew who the **SPECIAL GUESTS** were!

If it's NOT **DUDE 3** ... who can it be? Mr Sprocket and Mrs Nap are not saying a word at the run-through.

They tell me...
"You'll have to wait and see like everyone else, Tom."
Which is **irritating.** Because I wanted to go home and tell Delia that **DUDE3** were coming to our concert tonight. She's not going out much because of her (slightly) **GREEN** hair.
But it would still annoy her to miss them. And I would remind her how she'd missed them ... a lot.
Ha!
Oh well ... it can't be **DUDE3**, can it? Norman **MUST** have got that wrong.

At lunchtime Joey comes to find me and he says he's got a finished film of us playing "WILD THING".

"I'll ask my mum to send it to you, it's really good." ☺

(I am a GENIUS for getting Joey as a buddy – OK, I know he picked me, but it's still worked out well.)

High five

Because of the school production, **everybody** is allowed to go home an hour earlier to get ready.

Which doesn't take me and Derek long to do.

BEFORE

AFTER

Derek is round at my house and we're looking at some copies of **ROCK WEEKLY** when I suggest that if we're going to look more like a **ROCK** band, I should wear some "shades 👓

or **SPIKE** up my hair ... like this?"

And he says, "Do you think so?"
It might be a good idea.

I go into the bathroom and
help myself to some hair gel
that's been there for a while.
I think Uncle Kevin bought
it as a present for Dad ... as
a **joke.**
I still have a selection
of Delia's
sunglasses that we can
"borrow" for tonight, which both Derek and I
think we look pretty good in.

☺

Derek stays at mine for some dinner and while we're eating, Dad comes in holding a plastic bag. He says, "I've got myself some new shorts for running."

Which he's pleased about.

I whisper to Derek, "Let's hope Rooster's still hungry." Which makes him laugh.

TALENT → SHOW TONIGHT

(PLUS SPECIAL GUESTS!)

Chat

Chat

All the kids that are performing tonight are getting ready in the classrooms near the hall. There's a **lot** of excited chatting going on before the show starts. Me, Derek and Norman are all wearing our **DOGZOMBIES** T-shirts.

I show Norman the hair gel and say, "I think I should spike up my hair to look cooler and more like a

ROCK STAR"

And **AMY**, who's with Florence, hears me and says, "You should do it, Tom! That would look really good!" Norman just says,

YEAH!

because he's already getting a bit twitchy (like he does).

So I get a big handful of hair gel and put it in my hair, where it stays in a big

BLOB.

Derek says, "I think you need to rub it in a bit."

Which I do. "What now?"

AMY and Florence are looking at my hair. Florence says, "Maybe you should spike it up using a brush?"

But I don't have one. AMY says I can borrow her brush, which is nice of her. Now I've got half a TON of hair gel in my hair, I must look a bit silly.

Derek suggests I

go and find a mirror so you can see what you're doing.

(Good thinking.) I head to the toilet and try to SPIKE up my hair using AMY's funny little round brush.

I've never used one of these before.

I twiddle it round the front of my hair, then try and drag it up^{wards} into a **SPIKE**.

But it's **STUCK**. So I twist it round a bit more. Which doesn't work at all. This is NOT good. I'm trying not to **PANIC**. But the more I twist the brush, the more tangled up it gets.

This is turning out to be a **DISASTER!**

I'm taking so long that Derek comes to find me.

He says, "We need to get ready now, Tom." And I say, "There's a tiny bit of a problem."

And Derek says, "I know, Mr Sprocket wants us to go on early because of Marcus."

I don't think Derek has realized that the brush I'm holding in my hand is actually STUCK. I keep trying to get the brush out while asking,

"What's the problem with Marcus?"

Derek says, "Mr Sprocket wants us to perform FIRST because Marcus has got..."

I say,

"Nervous? ... Cold feet? ...

More annoying than ever?"

Derek says,

"No, not quite. He's cancelled because he's

got..."

"A bit of a ."

(Marcus scratching.)

Derek tells me his mum called and said it's [not] serious, but Marcus says he can't do his tricks because he's all ITCHY.

itchy →

(Marcus on SPORTS DAY)

That explains a lot.

Finally, Derek notices the brush sticking out of the top of my hair.

"What's wrong with your hair, Tom?"

"The brush is stuck,"

I say.

Derek has a go at trying to pull the brush out. I say "AGHHHH!" so he stops.

"How did you do THAT?"

"I twisted the brush and now it's stuck ... the hair gel made it worse."

I need to get help ... ≡ *FAST!*

But no one knows what to do.

Not even Mr Sprocket or Mrs Nap can get the brush out of my hair.

Mrs Mumble comes over. She says, "Joey got a comb stuck JUST like that."

"How did you get the comb out, Mrs Mumble?"

Mrs Mumble makes a `scissor-cutting`

movement with her fingers.

"His mum had to cut the comb out.

It was the only way, I'm afraid."

That's just great, then. GROAN...

Mr Sprocket says that we can go

on later if I need the time to sort out the

brush.

I say, "YES – we need LOADS more time."

(Like a WEEK.)

Mr Sprocket says I will have to get my mum

or dad to help now. Derek says he could go

and look for my mum in the audience if I

want.

"They should be here by now?"

Reluctantly, I say OK.

Mum takes one look at me and the brush and says, "How did you manage to do **that**, Tom?" I say, "It's a mystery, I just brushed my hair." (I don't mention the half ton of hair gel.)

AMY is feeling a bit guilty because it was her idea to use the brush.

She says, "I don't need it back if you have to **BREAK** it."

I really hope Mum's not going to do THAT!

Hi ya!

But the only pair of scissors that anyone can find to cut my hair with are a bit **BLUNT,** with round tips that are meant for paper.

Mum says, "I CAN'T use those, Tom."

So I have to either:

o   Ignore the brush (bit tricky).

o   Wear a BIG hat.

o   Wear a mask.

I don't want to go on stage with this brush **BOUNCING** around on my head.

The **TALENT** show has already started and seems to be going OK without Marcus.

Mr Keen made an announcement that there might be a few changes to the running order of the show.

We're now going to play LAST, so I'm hoping my hairbrush problem will be ALL sorted by then.

But it's not looking good.

Ta da!

Norman and Derek are shaking their heads and staring at me.

"This isn't working, is it, Tom?" Derek says.

He's right.

I don't want to go and play "**WILD THING**" in front of the school with a BRUSH sticking out of my hair.

I tell Mr Sprocket and Mrs Nap that I'm REALLY sorry, but I won't be able to play now.

"Never mind, Tom, We'll get the SPECIAL GUESTS to go on earlier," Mrs Nap says.

I'm thinking this could actually turn out to be really GREAT, because Mrs Nap knows I'm a **DUDE 3** fan. I ask her, "Are **DUDE 3** coming to play, then?" and she says, "That would be telling!"

Which probably means NO.

Mum goes back to her seat to watch the rest of the show (even though I'm not playing any more). She says she'll deal with the brush when I get home. (Shame.)

At least I get to watch the other talent-show performances that I didn't see before.

Like Mark Clump and his talking budgie.

Florence, **AMY** and Indrani singing.

(They're really good!)

Brad Galloway's EXCELLENT dancing.

Some little kids each doing

a line from a poem

(which takes a bit of time).

♪ A few more singers.

And **A**ctors.

And a **V**entriloquist.

(My favourite so far.)

When the last performance is over, Mr Keen comes on and all the lights go down.

He says it's been a wonderful show with SO many talented children from Oakfield School. *Clap*

"I'm sure you're all wondering who the **SPECIAL GUESTS** are tonight?"

Clap

Clap

Clap YESSSSSSSSS!

"Well, we are VERY privileged to welcome a WORLD-FAMOUS band to our school for a one-off performance – for the very first and possibly the LAST time."

And I'm looking at Derek and Norman, who've come to see who it is as well.

Norman says, Told you **DUDE3** were coming.

But I can't see them anywhere. Then Mr Keen says,

"We need to give a BIG OAKFIELD SCHOOL WELCOME to the one and only..."

(Drum rolllllllllllllllllllllll ... keep rolllllingggggggggggg...)

"YOU3!"

And for a split second I think Mr Keen has
said and I'm jumping up and
down and cheering when I see ...

Leather
trousers

Mr Fullerman, Mr Sprocket and MrsWorthingtash,
dressed like they're going to ride motorbikes.
Mrs Worthington has on a FALSE MOUSTACHE
(well, I hope it's false).
Me, Norman and Derek look SHOCKED.
Like this...

They start singing...

Get your lesson ready
Head out to the classroom
Get the children running
Practising for SPORTs DAY

We're a NEW teachers' band
Who are born to be MILD
We can keep our cool
In Oakfield School

BORN TO BE MILD.

BORN TO BE MILD.

It's a funny song ... some of the adults are LAUGHING extra hard!

Mr Sprocket and Mr Fullerman are stomping around pretending to be ROCK stars. But it's MRS WORTHINGTON who's going CRAZY!

I say to Derek, "This is the MADDEST thing ever!"

It might not be DUDE 3, but You3 are so hilarious I almost forget about the brush stuck in my hair.

Then the WHOLE school clap and Cheer when they finish playing.

CLAP! Hooray CLAP! Hooray

I think the kids in our school will be talking about this teachers' performance
FOR EVER!

Thank you and goodnight

Now the show's over I say bye to everyone and go and meet up with Mum and Dad, who both think the teachers' band was "VERY good!" Dad says, "Makes me want to be in a band!"

Mum gives him a look ☉☉ and says, "I don't think so."

(I agree with Mum.)

At least Dad has brought the car so I don't have to walk home with this ══▓▓▓ brush sticking out of my hair. (Which is a relief.)

I can avoid people STARING at me, wondering what I've done.
I can't avoid Delia, though. When we get home, Mum and Dad are even telling Delia how FUNNY the teachers' band was.

Delia isn't listening. She's too busy looking at me and shaking her head.

She says,

 "How did you do that, idiot?"

 So I say, "It was an accident – bit like your **GREEN** hair. Mum's going to help sort it out now."

But before I get the chance to think about what Mum is ACTUALLY going to do (CUT the brush out), she suddenly appears with some scissors

and does this...
SNIP! SNIP!

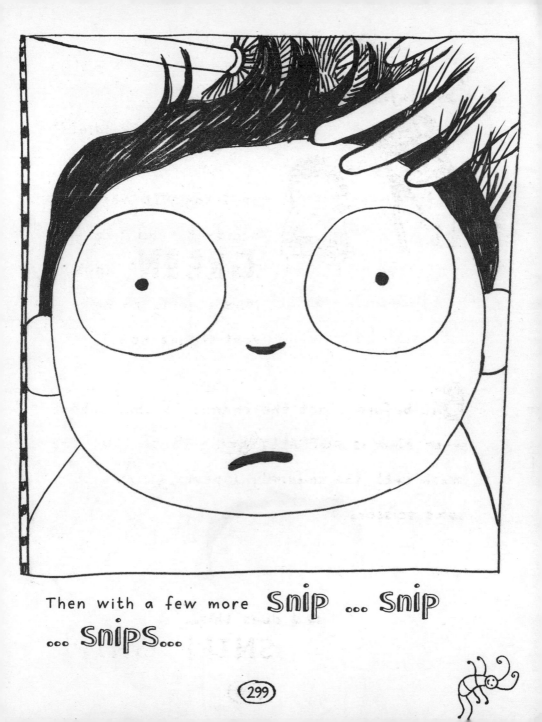

Then with a few more Snip ... Snip ... SnipS...

It's all finished. I keep my eyes closed until
Mum says, "There, all gone now."

I go and take a look in the mirror to see
what Mum's done.

And she's right...
It really is all gone now.

Gulp.

Delia catches me looking at my hair. I'm just waiting for her to say something HORRID as usual when she says,

"Don't worry, it will grow back ... eventually."

Which isn't the *worst* thing she could have said, I suppose?

I go upstairs to get ready for bed, then remember to let Derek know the important news – I do a quick doodle and put it up at my window.

NEWS FLASH

THE HAIRBRUSH IS GONE

(and so is some of my hair).

Mum and Dad both come in to say goodnight.

They tell me my hair looks very cool shorter.

(I'm not so sure.)

I think it looks a bit odd?

So I'm lying in bed, sort of going to sleep. But I can't stop thinking about:

1. **YOU3** – so funny!

2. My CHOPPED-off hair.

If I have to sit next to Marcus (when he stops itching and comes back to school) with my hair like this, he'll probably just keep making stupid jokes all the time.

Which will drive me

BONKERS.

Did you cut your hair
with a knife and fork?

Hair today
gone tomorrow

Then all of a sudden, I get one of MY
VERY BEST-ever ideas that comes to
me in a *FLASH.*

I jump out of bed quickly and grab a comb.

Until my hair grows back a bit more, I could just do this?

Let's see if it works...

ANOTHER...

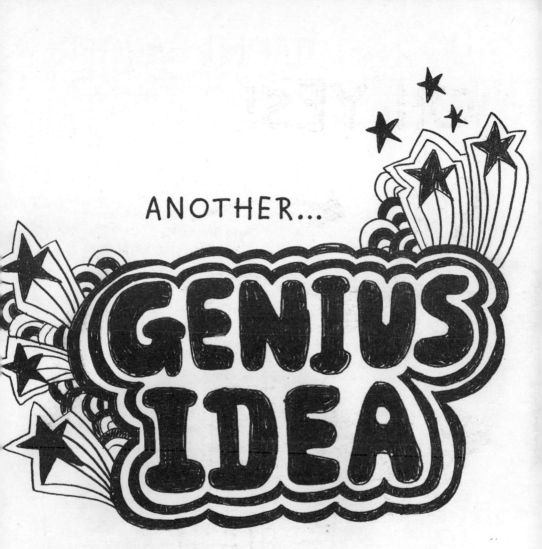

GENIUS IDEA

If I do say so myself...

(Thank you ... thank you.)

How to make a PAPER BANGER

1 A3 paper.

2 Fold in half.

make the corners meet up

3 Then fold in quarters.

4 Then UNFOLD the paper. There should be nice fold marks now.

5 Fold down the corner to meet the middle fold line.

6 Do the same with every corner.

7

8 Your paper should look like this.

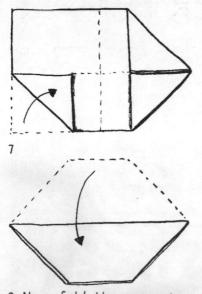

9 Now fold the paper in half, with the flaps inside.

10 Fold the right corner to the middle.

11 Then repeat on the other side.

12 Fold the whole banger in half, hold the corners marked, then flick it down HARD.

Air catches under here to make a BANG!

BANG!

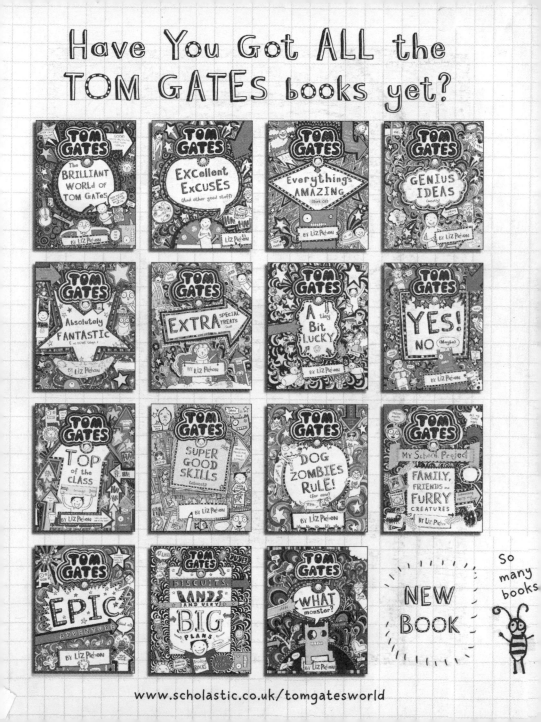

It's just as well that Joey took some other film for our video because the one that Mr Fingle helped set up didn't really work.

For obvious reasons...

This is what our video from Mr Fingle did look like

GENIUS at:
- Most things
- Ignoring Marcus
- Remembering everything

TOM GATES

GENIUS at:
- Being very clever in class
- Being super good at sports day
- AND in the talent show (sigh)

AMY PORTER

GENIUS at:
- Hearing everything
- Bin liner recycling
- Map reading

RITA GATES

GENIUS at:
- Sprinting around
- Jumping
- Dancing with 6 legs

DANCING BUG